How Can You Hijack a Cave?

Also by P. J. Petersen

How Can You Hijack a Cave?

P. J. Petersen

Delacorte
Press

Published by
Delacorte Press
The Bantam Doubleday Dell Publishing Group, Inc.
666 Fifth Avenue
New York, New York 10103

Library of Congress Cataloging in Publication Data
Petersen, P. J.
How can you hijack a cave?
Summary: Two teenage tour guides at the Cathedral Caverns try
to rescue a friend being held in a cave by kidnappers demand-
ing money for her release.
[1. Kidnapping—Fiction. 2. Caves—Fiction]
I. Title.
PZ7.P44197Ho   1988   [Fic]   88-7139
ISBN 0-440-50063-X

Manufactured in the United States of America

November 1988

10 9 8 7 6 5 4 3 2 1

BG

For Carla, my favorite basketball player

How Can You Hijack a Cave?

July 16—5:47 P.M.

The cave door flew open. "Help!" A man dashed into the sunlight, waving his arms. "Help!"

Curt unbuckled the first aid kit from the dashboard. It was probably a twisted ankle. Or maybe a fainting spell. He yanked the kit free and stepped off the bus.

By then people were swarming down the stairs toward him. Curt raced to the bottom of the stairs. "What's the matter?" he yelled.

"Call the police!" the man shouted.

"What happened?"

The man stopped in front of Curt and shouted, "Call the police! It's terrorists!"

"What?"

The man swore through closed teeth. "Terrorists. They've got guns and hand grenades. Hurry up and call the police!"

"There's no phone up here," Curt said.

"You mean there's no radio on that bus?" the man screamed. "What's the matter with you people?"

"Get out of the way," a woman said, pushing past the man and running toward the bus.

"Is anybody hurt up there?" Curt asked.

"No." The man turned and followed the others. "Seems like you'd have something—"

Curt watched the people rush past. "Everybody on the bus," he said. It was a stupid thing to say. They were already pushing and shoving to get on board.

"Here," a gray-haired woman said. "You better take these." She shoved some papers into Curt's hand and trotted on.

Curt glanced at them, two sheets of ordinary white paper covered with block letters. He read the first few lines, then ran toward the bus.

He pushed past a man on the steps and slid into the driver's seat. A woman leaned forward and said, "Our guide's still up there."

Curt mashed on the starter. "I know."

"There's one of them," somebody yelled.

Curt leaned close to the windshield so that he could see the mouth of the cave. A bulky figure in dark clothes was pulling the door shut.

"Oh, my!" a woman said after the figure was gone. "I thought he was coming after us." A few people snickered.

Curt released the clutch with a jerk. He was disgusted with himself. He was going to have to tell the police about seeing the person, and he had nothing to tell. The figure could have been male or female, tall or short. Curt was going to turn out to be one of those unreliable witnesses that he always read about.

Out of habit, he flipped on the microphone. The usual procedure was to tell three jokes about the winding road and the hundred-foot dropoff below it: "If you folks are in a hurry, we could always take the shortcut."

He saw the pale faces in his mirror and flipped off the microphone. What was there to say to people who had just seen their guide get kidnapped?

Speeding was out of the question. He took the turns

at seven miles an hour instead of the usual five and felt the rear wheels slide.

"I thought we were done for," a woman said. Nobody answered her.

After the first series of turns, Curt flipped on the microphone again. His voice came out higher than he expected. "How many people are still in the cave?"

Several people answered, some saying "One," others saying "Three." A man leaned forward and said, "There were two of them. Fat guys with beards and sunglasses. They let everybody go except the guide. I thought they'd keep all of us, but they just kept that one little girl. Doesn't make much sense, but I guess I shouldn't complain."

Curt nodded and set down the microphone. Keeping just the one girl did make sense, although he didn't bother to explain that. The girl was Pauline Thomas, whose father was worth at least ten million dollars.

As he steered the bus around the last big turn, Curt spoke into the microphone again. "Folks, when we get to the store, I'd appreciate it if you'd all stay on the bus. I'll call the sheriff and see what he wants us to do." Somebody muttered about having people waiting, and a woman asked how long he thought it would take. Curt pretended not to hear. He pulled the bus next to the curb and dashed into the building.

Lori was filling paper cups with ice as he came through the door. "You're early." Then, "What's the matter?"

"Big trouble," Curt shouted. He grabbed the phone and punched 911. "Some nuts have Pauline up in the cave."

Lori dropped her scoop into the ice bin and headed around the counter. Curt handed her the papers.

Curt talked to an emergency operator and three deputies before somebody located the sheriff. "All right," the sheriff said in the calmest voice Curt had heard in the last twenty minutes, "we've got men on their way out there. I want you to read me that note."

When Curt finished reading, the sheriff let out a groan. "I'll be out myself right away. You make sure nobody leaves before my men get there."

"Everybody's still on the bus," Curt said.

"Good. Now, Curtis. That's what you said, isn't it?"

"Yes, sir. Curt Carver."

"All right, Curtis. It's been a while since I was out there at Cathedral Caverns. That thing's a dead end, isn't it? You've got that twisty bus road up to the cave and just the one entrance, right?"

"That's right," Curt said.

"That's what I thought. So those boys aren't going anywhere."

"No, sir."

"This whole thing is crazy." The sheriff sighed and asked the question that was going to be asked hundreds of times in the next few hours: "How can you hijack a cave?"

2

On the first trip he ever made to Cathedral Caverns, Curt walked the whole six miles from Barker Mills. At first he had smiled and stuck out his thumb whenever a car passed, but it was a waste of time. Nobody was going to stop for a 6'8" hitchhiker, even if he did have a big stupid grin on his face.

Curt hadn't really expected a ride. Nothing else had gone right since he had left Bolivia three days ago. Why should this be any different?

Thanks to flight delays and missed connections, he had arrived at the Barker Mills bus depot at 4:00 A.M., eighteen hours late. He should have called Coach Franks right then, but he hated the idea of bothering anybody at that hour. So he had stretched out on a wooden bench to wait.

When he had called at seven and a sleepy woman answered after the sixth ring, he knew he hadn't waited long enough. "You're the Carver boy?" she asked after hearing his name twice. "Jim's off on a fishing trip. I guess he gave up on you. He expected you yesterday, and then you didn't call or anything." Curt started to explain, but she didn't seem to hear. "He said for you to see the people at Cathedral Caverns about a job. You can take a taxi out there."

A taxi was out of the question, but Curt had thanked her and hung up. The woman already thought he was a clod. He wasn't about to tell her that he had arrived from South America with less than a dollar in his pocket.

Curt left his luggage with the station clerk, who gave him directions to the caverns. Soon he was marching along the shoulder of Highway 126, his arms swinging in an easy rhythm. After being cooped up on airplanes and buses, he was glad to be in the open air, moving on his own.

This was his first chance to look around. He hadn't been in the United States for five years, and he was fascinated by everything around him—the twisted oak trees, the silver mailboxes, the pickup trucks, even the soft-drink cans and gum wrappers in the ditch.

At the turnoff to Cathedral Caverns, he stopped to tuck in his shirt and comb his hair. He wondered if he should have worn a tie. If he was dressed wrong, he could always tell them that his luggage had been lost.

He took a deep breath and marched down the long driveway. His stomach had turned into a rock, the way it always did before a big game. He stopped at the edge of the parking lot and checked his hair again. A few cars sat in front of a log cabin with a huge WELCOME TO CATHEDRAL CAVERNS sign on its roof. At the side of the cabin, people were boarding a sky-blue school bus. Curt strode toward the cabin door, a broad smile on his face.

That big empty smile was the first thing he'd learned in Bolivia. When people screamed at him in a language he didn't understand, he flashed that smile and held his ground. Soon the smile became automatic. He would have used it to greet a hungry lion or a firing squad.

"Hey there." A blond girl beside the bus waved at him. "If you hurry up, you can still make the tour."

"That's okay."

The girl jogged over to him. She was one of the tallest girls he had ever seen, but she had the easy stride of a distance runner. "We can wait for you," she said. "The next tour won't leave for another hour." She was wearing a sweatshirt that read I SURVIVED THE BUS RIDE AT CATHEDRAL CAVERNS.

"I'm not here for the tour," Curt said. "I need to see the man in charge."

"I'm the man in charge. Only, you may have noticed, I'm not a man."

Curt swallowed but managed to say, "I definitely noticed." He was surprised when the girl didn't smile.

She glanced toward the bus. "We're on a tight schedule. What can I do for you?"

"Coach Franks said you might have a job opening."

She looked him over quickly. "Oh, you're the guy from Brazil, huh?"

"Bolivia."

"Whatever. Look, I've got to get this tour going. I'll talk to you in an hour. Go inside and get some coffee or something." She turned her back and jogged toward the bus.

Curt stood on the steps of the cabin and watched the bus chug up a narrow gravel road. He could hear the engine whining long after the bus disappeared into the trees. He checked the change in his pocket and wondered if he could get a cup of coffee for forty-seven cents.

Inside was a souvenir shop, with racks of postcards and shelves crammed with mugs and ashtrays. To the right of the entrance was a snack bar. A stocky woman behind the cash register called out, "Good morning. You just missed the tour."

"I know. I talked to the girl out there. Is she really the boss?"

"Lori? She's the boss, all right. Only she knows better than to boss me. She's running the place this summer while her mom's going to summer school in Alaska."

"I'm supposed to see her when she comes back. Coach Franks sent me out here."

"So you're the one, huh? Franks was around last week giving us a real sales pitch about you. He figures he can win the league with you on the team. Said your father was the best basketball player he ever coached." She glanced at Curt. "And I suppose you're a chip off the old block."

Curt kept smiling. "I'm not as good as my father. Just ask him."

The woman grinned and leaned against the cash register. "How'd you get tied up with Franks? He an old friend or something?"

"I've never even met him," Curt said. "I need a year of American high school to get ready for college, and he said he'd help me out."

"I'll bet he did. He's got a real soft spot in his heart for guys your size." She shrugged. "Well, Curtis, Coach Franks gives me a pain, but we could use somebody like you around the place. Some of these sticky-fingered types see you, and they might think twice before they start filling their pockets." She smiled at Curt. "You lift weights, don't you?"

Curt nodded. "Everybody who plays ball for my dad is on a training program."

"I thought so. Nobody gets muscles like that by accident. I'm Wanda, by the way." She reached across the counter and shook his hand with a solid grip.

"Curt Carver."

Wanda opened a drawer. "I guess you might as well fill out an application while you're waiting. If it was up to me, I'd hire you right now, but I guess we'd better go by the book." She pushed a form toward him. "You need a pen?"

"Yes, ma'am."

"Don't call me ma'am, Curt. I feel old enough as it is."

Curt leaned over the counter and filled in his name. After that, he was stuck. What was he supposed to use for an address? And the next boxes called for job experience and personal references—complete with blanks for more addresses and phone numbers he didn't have. He flashed his smile and pushed the form away.

"What's the matter?" Wanda asked.

"I don't have anything to put down. I've been living in Bolivia for the past five years."

"You could always make something up. That's what most people do on these applications." She glanced at the form. "Didn't you do any work down there?"

"Sure, but I don't have the addresses and the phone numbers."

"Make 'em up. I guarantee you nobody is going to call Bolivia to check. What kind of work did you do?"

Curt shrugged. "All the rotten jobs—I cleared brush, dug holes, carried equipment. My dad wanted to be sure that I wasn't being treated special, so he always gave me the jobs nobody else wanted."

"I thought you said your father was a basketball coach."

"That's what he does while he's resting. He's also an engineer and a teacher and I don't know what else."

"Does he work for the government?"

"He works for anybody. Half the time he's not even getting paid. He went down there as a civil engineer, but he says that in a country like Bolivia, it's stupid just to build something. He wants to teach people how to build things for themselves. So he works with people on projects—bridges, sewer systems, roads, housing projects."

"I see. Coach Franks said something about that, but I thought he was just blowing smoke." She looked at Curt. "He said your dad was an amazing guy—kind of a one-man Peace Corps."

Curt smiled and shook his head. "I guess. He's also crabby and hot-tempered and hard to live with."

"Most of us amazing people are like that." She smiled and pushed the application form toward him. "Just write down that you were an administrative assistant. Or an apprentice engineer. That's close enough. Then give your dad as your employer."

Curt picked up the pen. "How about nuclear physicist, astronaut, and rock star?"

"Don't push your luck."

The door swung open, and an elderly couple in matching T-shirts came inside. "Good morning," Wanda called out. "Let me help these people," she told Curt. "Then I'll get back to you."

Curt headed for the bookrack. He grabbed a book about caves and flipped through it. He wondered if he should admit he'd never been inside a cave before. Or maybe he could fake it. While Wanda sold tickets to the couple in T-shirts and to another family, he memorized the difference between a stalactite (growing down from the top) and a stalagmite (growing up from the bottom).

He was reading about bats when Wanda called, "Hey, Curtis Duane Carver, come over here."

Curt replaced his book and walked to the counter. "Where'd those people go?"

"I sent them out on our nature trail. We have it all set up with signs and displays. It gives people something to do while they're waiting for the tour." She pushed the application to one side. "Now let's get to the important stuff. You're not a smoker, are you?"

"No."

"Good. Two things I can't stand—smokers and fanatics."

"Fanatics?"

"Look, Curtis, I don't care what people believe or what they eat or what they do when I'm not around. Just so they don't try to convert me. We had a girl working here last summer that drove me nuts. Wanted to turn me into a vegetarian. Made a face every time I ate a hot dog. It got so I was eating hot dogs all day long just to get her goat. I put on fifteen pounds, and it was all her fault."

"I like hot dogs," Curt said.

"Not me. After last summer I can't stand the sight of 'em."

Curt looked at Wanda. "I'm a fanatic about girls and ice cream and basketball, but if you'll help me get the job, I promise I won't try to convert you."

"I'd rather have somebody who was a fanatic about mopping floors and cleaning toilets, but I guess you'll do."

"You really think I ought to fill out that application?" he asked.

Wanda shrugged. "Suit yourself."

"I don't want to make any more mistakes," Curt said. "I already fouled things up by telling that girl I wanted to see the man in charge."

Wanda laughed. "That must have gone over big."

"Yeah."

She leaned across the counter. "Do you know what you're getting into, Curtis? You ready to scrub bathrooms and pick up cigarette butts? You ready to keep smiling at people who deserve to have their fannies kicked? You ready to be bossed around by three women? And we're all ornery."

"I've been doing crummy jobs all my life. I'll survive." The empty smile was back on his face again.

"You sure this is how you want to spend your summer?"

Curt took a deep breath and let it go. "What difference does it make what I want?" He forced himself to keep smiling. "Look, I have forty-seven cents in my pocket, and that's it. That cuts down on my choices."

Wanda reached across the counter for the application form. She wadded it up and tossed it into the wastebasket beside her. "You want something to eat, Curt? How about a roll and some coffee?"

"Should I be polite and say no?"

"Not with me."

"I'll take it, then. Thank you."

Wanda brought him two cinnamon rolls and a banana on a paper plate, then poured him some coffee. "You really down to forty-seven cents?"

Curt nodded. "I didn't have much extra, and then the bus ticket cost a lot more than we figured."

"I want you to remember this food, Curt. When you get to be one of these rich basketball stars driving around in your silver Rolls-Royce, you remember the old lady that fed you, all right? You can send me some spare change once in a while."

By the time Curt finished eating, a dozen people were wandering along the aisles. Curt put his plate in a garbage can and went back to the bookrack. He spent a few minutes reading about claustrophobia—a pathological fear of confined spaces, the book called it—and wondered if he would get it. Sometimes little rooms with low ceilings bothered him. How would he feel inside a cave?

Hearing tires squeal, Curt looked out the window to see a red Corvette skid to a stop in the parking lot. A small dark-haired girl dashed toward the store, jerked open the door, then walked calmly to the cash register. "I'm sorry, Wanda," she whispered.

"You're late, and you're sorry," Wanda said. "So what's new?" She waved Curt over. "This is Pauline. She works here—sometimes. Pauline, this is Curt. He's crazy enough to think he wants to be part of this outfit."

Pauline smiled up at him. "Hi, Curt. Coach Franks told us all about you."

"If he said good things, they're all true," Curt said. Pauline reminded him of the prettiest Bolivian girls— glossy black hair and sparkling dark eyes. And, just like the Bolivian girls, the top of her head barely reached his rib cage.

"The drinks are all set," Wanda told Pauline. "Make the bus call." She motioned Curt closer and said, "We give everybody a free lemonade at the end of the tour. That brings 'em back in here so that they'll buy stuff."

Pauline picked up a microphone from beside the register. "Ladies and gentlemen, our tour will be leaving in about three minutes. Please follow me through the front door to the waiting area. If you haven't bought your ticket, you still have time to do so." She set down the microphone and looked at Curt. "I'm glad you're here. We've been really swamped."

"I haven't been hired yet," he said.

Pauline reached out and squeezed his arm. "I wouldn't worry if I were you." She winked and headed for the door.

In thirty seconds Curt and Wanda were the only ones left inside. "Look at her," Wanda said. Curt stepped to the window and watched Pauline waving her arms as she marched up and down in front of the others. "You can learn a lot from her. She's probably done five hundred tours, but she's bubbling over like this was her first trip. That's important."

"She looks like she's having fun."

"She'd better look that way. Even if she's ready to kill the whole bunch. You see, Curtis, this isn't Carlsbad Caverns. What we've got here is a nice run-of-the-mill cave. Nobody's going to fall over dead when they see it. But if we're excited and if we make the whole trip fun, people feel like they got their money's worth."

"Show business," Curt said.

"Exactly. And nobody knows it better than that little monkey out there."

The blue bus made a circle in the parking lot and chugged to a stop beside the store. "You have any good last-minute advice for me?" Curt asked Wanda.

"Just relax," Wanda said. "Lori's never hired anybody before, so I don't know exactly how she'll handle things. Just be straight with her, and you'll do fine."

Curt stood at the window and watched Lori trot down the steps of the bus. She stood to the side and handed out tickets, laughing and talking with the people. Then she trotted into the store and shouted at Curt, "I'll be with you in a little while." She headed behind the counter and took tickets while Wanda passed out lemonade.

The speed of the operation amazed Curt, who was used to the relaxed methods of the Bolivians. In less than three minutes the people from the bus were in the store sipping their lemonade, and the bus, loaded again, was rumbling up the hill with Pauline at the wheel. He wondered why they needed him.

Lori left the counter and headed toward Curt. "I'm Lori Matlock," she said, shoving a hand in his direction.

"Curt Carver." He took her hand, wondering what she'd do if he kissed it, the way a Bolivian gentleman would. It would be an interesting way not to get hired.

Lori gave his hand a quick squeeze and let it go. "Hold on a few more minutes, okay?" She turned away before he could answer.

Curt stood back and watched Lori circulate among the customers, helping a boy find a sweatshirt in his size, opening a locked cabinet to bring out watches, teasing a man who was trying on a hat. He wondered if she was as confident as she seemed and decided that she probably was.

When most of the customers had left, Lori opened a door at the rear of the store and called, "Hey, come on."

He jogged toward her. "What's back here?"

"My house—among other things." She led the way through a storage room, where the shelves were jammed with cardboard cartons. She grabbed a basketball off a shelf and flipped it to him without looking back. He managed not to drop it. She opened another door and stepped into the sunlight. "Let's see if you're as good as Coach Franks said you were."

"He's never seen me play." Curt blinked his eyes against the bright sun. In the trees to his right were a white cottage and some outbuildings, but he hardly noticed them. Directly in front of him was a black-topped basketball court with freshly painted white lines. At the far end of the paved area was a metal pole with a regulation backboard. "This is some setup."

Lori snatched the ball out of his hands. "All right. Loser's outs. Twenty points wins. That okay with you?"

Curtis stared at her. "You want to play right now?"

"Sure. What's the matter?"

Curt glanced down at his black leather street shoes. "Nothing, I guess."

"Then let's move it," Lori said. "You want to shoot free throws to see who takes it out first?"

He wondered how hard he should play. Would he blow his chance for a job if he made her look bad? But she couldn't really expect him to let her win, could she? "Go ahead. You take it."

"Your funeral." Her smooth dribble surprised him. She kept her head high and her body square. His father, a fanatic about fundamentals, would have loved her. Before Curt got his hands in the air, she stopped at the free-throw line and sent a jump shot through the basket without touching the rim.

"Good shot." He walked over and picked up the ball.

"Hustle it up," Lori said. "We only have a few minutes."

Curt jogged to the back of the court, then began dribbling toward the basket. Lori darted toward him, her hand outstretched. Without thinking, he stopped dribbling and pivoted away from her. "Dumb," he muttered. There he was—twenty feet from the basket, with nothing to do but shoot. Lori moved in close, her hands high. He made a halfhearted fake and put up a fade-away jumper that careened off the front rim.

Lori caught the ball and dribbled beyond the free-throw line. He moved in close. He wasn't going to give her another easy jump shot. She jerked her head up, and he leaped high, his hands ready for the block. But the shot didn't come. Instead, she dribbled right past him and laid the ball in the basket.

"Nice move," he told her, forcing himself to smile. She was a good ballplayer—he'd give her that. But he was doing a terrible job. His father would have benched him for a stupid move like that.

"Four–zip," she called out.

Curt wasn't about to make another mistake. He kept his body between her and the ball while he maneuvered close to the basket. He shot an easy eight-footer.

Lori hit another jump shot and called out, "Six–two."

"You want to talk about the job?" Curt asked her.

"Later," she said. "This is getting interesting."

Again Curt worked in close to the basket. He faked to the left and went up for a shot. His hands went high, but the ball was gone. Lori streaked to the basket for an easy lay-up. "Eight–two. I don't have to clear it on a stolen ball."

Curt grabbed the ball and dribbled beyond the free-throw line. "I'm a little rusty," he muttered.

"Now the excuses start."

"I wasn't making excuses," he answered, too loud.

"Could have fooled me."

Curt pivoted to his right, leaped high, and slammed the ball through the basket.

Lori picked up the ball and looked at him. "I've never seen anybody dunk before," she said. "Except on television, of course." She began to dribble again.

"Well, it makes a good show, but it still only counts two points. Eight–four."

"Let's go," Curt said. The dunk had settled him down. Now he had to start playing real basketball. When Lori began to dribble, he moved in close. He kept his eyes on her shoulders, and he kept his feet on the ground. When she went up for a shot, he leaped with her and batted the ball away.

"Foul!" she yelled.

He hadn't touched her, but he wasn't about to argue with the boss. He shrugged and tossed the ball to her. "Sorry."

She threw the ball back—hard. "Don't give me that. It was a clean block, and you know it. You got all ball."

Curt waved her away. "You called the foul, not me."

She glared at him. "What do you expect me to say when you stuff me? Should I thank you for making me look bad?" She took a step toward him. "Look, I want you to play just as hard as you can. If I beat you, I don't want you to go around saying, 'I was just fooling around.'"

Curt laughed. "First you have to beat me."

Lori almost smiled. "You going to stand there, or are you going to play ball?"

The score was sixteen–fourteen, her favor, when Wanda's voice came over the loudspeaker: "Lori, you'd better get in here. We're starting to get crowded."

Lori stopped dribbling and tossed the ball to Curt. "You've got some bad habits," she said, "but you're a pretty good jumper." She turned her back and headed for the cabin.

"Just a second," Curt called out.

She looked over her shoulder. "What's the matter?"

"When can we talk about the job?"

"You're hired," Lori said. "I really need to play somebody like you. I have to learn to handle people taller than I am."

"And that's the job?"

Lori gave him a disgusted look. "You're dreaming."

"Well—" he began.

"Look, we need another guide for the cave. Basketball is for in-between times." She yanked open the door to the storage room. "Just come along with me and see how we do things. Right now we'd better get in there and keep our eyes open. Basketball's only the number two sport around here. Number one is shoplifting." She looked back at him. "You did say you'd take the job, didn't you?"

"No," Curt said, shoving the basketball onto a shelf. He waited until her mouth started to open, then said, "But I will."

"Good," Lori said. "And the game's not over. It was sixteen–fourteen, my favor, and I had the ball."

3

Curt was soon settled into a comfortable routine. He slept in a loft above the bus garage and ate his meals with Lori and Wanda, who was staying at the Matlocks' house while Lori's mother was gone. Wanda was even teaching him to cook a little.

Whenever things were slow, Curt and Lori headed for the basketball court. She could be a real pain, but she was good for his game. If he made a sloppy move or a lazy fake, she would slap the ball away and announce it to the world: "Nice move, Grace" or "Classy play, Dufus."

When Curt wrote to his father, most of the letter was about these games. He didn't mention the scores, though. His father probably wouldn't believe that Curt had to be in top form to squeeze out a 20–16 win over a girl. He had to play tight but clean defense, which was tough against someone as quick as Lori. And he had to keep his temper. With Lori's fast hands and her even faster mouth, that was the hardest part of all.

The tours were easy enough. It had taken Curt a few days to memorize the cave spiel and a few more to make it sound natural. "You've got to develop your own style," Wanda had told him. "Lori sounds like a scientist, and Pauline sounds like a cheerleader, and I sound like the old lady of the mountain." Curt thought he sounded like a college professor, but Wanda said he came across as a good old boy.

Tours ran every hour, nine to five, seven days a week. At busy times they ran an extra tour on the half hour. Since they only had one bus, everybody had to stay on schedule by following The Plan.

When he gathered his tour group together outside the store, Curt told them what to expect: "We'll start with a flight of sixty-two steps. Then we'll be walking about half a mile inside the cave." This usually brought out a few groans, and once in a while somebody decided not to go.

When everybody was on the bus, he drove out of the parking lot and began a spiel about the history of the cave. This built up interest and took people's minds off the narrow gravel road they were taking up the mountain. On the way down he would make jokes about the steep dropoff, but the system called for keeping people calm on the way up.

At the turnaround he pointed out Barker Mills in the distance. That gave the people something to look at while he backed the bus into position. He then led the tour off the bus and up the sixty-two cement steps, stopping at the halfway point to tell about the natural opening, now sealed, at the top of the mountain. This stop gave people a chance to catch their breaths.

At the entrance to the cave came the explanation that this first section had been drilled by hard-rock miners and was the only nonnatural part of the cave. This speech gave people another short rest.

Then he had to make the most important decision of the tour. He had to pick somebody who would do exactly what he was told—usually a twelve-year-old boy or a middle-aged man. That person had to lead the group through a narrow tunnel, then turn left as soon as possible. Otherwise, the whole effect was spoiled.

The person to blame was a man named Tanner, who had originally opened Cathedral Caverns for tourists. Since the natural opening to the cave was too small and nearly inaccessible, Tanner had hired surveyors to figure out where to drill an entrance to the Cathedral Room, the one spectacular section. The surveyors had done their work accurately, and so had the hard-rock miners that Tanner hired. The shaft went straight into the main room. That was good engineering, but lousy show business. Once people saw that room, the rest of the cave was a disappointment.

So the secret was to get people to hurry past the unlighted main room without noticing what was there. That was why he needed a leader who would keep the group moving while Curt closed the door and brought up the rear.

In the first wide spot beyond the main room—which they called the Popcorn Room because of the cave coral on the walls—he would talk about the way stalactites were formed while he checked the people for signs of claustrophobia. Anybody who was starting to panic could be led back to the entrance without messing up the schedule too badly.

Then they made a quarter-mile loop past some nice rock draperies and a honey-colored flowstone formation they called Frozen Falls. At the end of the loop he had to lead them past the main room again, but this time he was in front and could hurry the group along. The section to the right of the big room was the least interesting section of the cave. The only unusual feature was the low ceiling, which meant that tall people had to duck. It also meant that Curt banged his head at least once a tour.

This section of the cave ended in the Pink Room, where he turned off the lights to let people experience total darkness. "We give 'em a little scare," Wanda had explained. "That way, they forget how boring that part is."

Then they went back through the same low passage and ended up in the Cathedral Room, where everybody oohed and aahed when he threw on the lights. He pointed out formations ("There's Popeye, and there's his can of spinach") and answered questions, keeping an eye on his watch. At thirteen minutes before the hour he took the group back through the tunnel and into the sunlight. On the way down the hill he joked about the road and the strange things they hadn't seen in the cave—like bats and cave spiders.

If nobody had stopped to tie a shoelace, he would pull into the loading zone about two minutes before the hour. He then passed out the free-drink coupons, helped customers, and kept an eye out for shoplifters.

Curt figured he had a soft touch—an easy job with plenty of time to play basketball. While other people suffered out in the sizzling heat, he was in an air-conditioned store or in a cave, where the temperature was always 58 degrees. The five-minute bus rides were just long enough to make him appreciate being inside the rest of the time.

The job had its bad points, but he could live with them. Now and then he had to listen to Lori's lectures on proper procedures, but he just put on his empty smile and waited for her to finish. The worst part, of course, was cleaning up after the slobs who spilled ice cream and dropped wads of gum and stuck their gooey hands on the windows. But at least everybody pitched in on the janitor work. Even Pauline, whose father owned the cave and the whole surrounding area. She was usually late for work—whipping into the parking lot in her red Corvette that was probably worth as much as the store—but once she arrived, she did her share.

Curt thought about the rich girls he had known in Bolivia. You wouldn't catch those spoiled little darlings scrubbing toilets and emptying ashtrays. And he had been spoiled just as rotten as any of them. He and his father had always had a maid. He would toss his dirty clothes into a corner, and the next day the clothes would show up in his dresser clean and pressed.

But he was learning, thanks to Wanda. The first time she handed him a toilet brush, she had realized that he didn't know what it was. "We've got to complete your education, Curtis," she said. "You can't afford to hire a cleaning woman on your salary." She had showed him how to use the washing machine, how to clean windows without leaving streaks, even how to sew buttons on his clothes.

He was proud of learning these things, even if he did crack jokes about making somebody a good wife. His friends in Bolivia wouldn't believe their eyes if they could see him in the kitchen with an apron around his waist, doing stir-fry vegetables, one of the first things Wanda had taught him.

This was a new country—even if it was his own—and he had to learn to live in it. He still couldn't believe some of the clothes he saw. People would get arrested in Bolivia for wearing things like that. And he was amazed at the way children talked to their parents in public. But he was an American, and he was glad to be home.

He still wasn't sure about American girls, though. He couldn't read their signals. Pauline was always putting her hands on his arms or shoulders, but it didn't mean anything. She had a steady boyfriend who had just left for West Point. Besides, she was so tiny that the two of them together were a walking joke.

Lori was probably the right size for him, although he still wasn't used to being around a girl that tall. Sometimes he thought he saw a gleam in her eye, but the only time she touched him was when she fouled him on the basketball court.

It was probably better that way. After all, she was the boss. And she was too serious for him. She had to have everything correct, in its place, and on schedule. She got upset when the tours ran five minutes late or the cash register total was off by a dime.

She even turned basketball into a job. She couldn't just go out and shoot baskets; she had to play a game. And the game had to be serious. She would get mad and walk off the court if he took a crazy shot just for the fun of it.

Early in his second week Pauline stayed after work and had dinner with them. Wanda cooked fried chicken, and Curt told crazy stories about playing basketball in Bolivia. Afterwards he and Pauline did the dishes, then wandered out to the basketball court.

They shot a few baskets while Pauline told him about Barker Mills High School. "It's going to be strange this year without Roger around," she said.

"Don't worry," Curt told her. "If you get bored, you and I can go out and do something exciting." He shot the ball. "If we can think of anything exciting to do in Barker Mills."

"We can always go cruising," Pauline said. "Three fascinating minutes from one end of town to the other."

"We may have to stop and rest halfway," he said, dribbling in a circle. "I can only take so much at once."

Lori opened the storage room door and shouted, "Who's ahead?"

"Here you go," Curt yelled. "Two seconds to go in the game. Desperation shot time." He threw her the ball. "One second. Bzz."

Lori sent the ball clear over the backboard.

"Not your night to be a hero," he said, trotting after the ball.

"Or a heroine," she said.

"Curt and I were just planning a big date," Pauline said. "We're going to cruise downtown Barker Mills. Maybe even have a Coke at the truck stop."

"You want to play a little two-on-one?" Lori said. "Let's make the South American flash work a little."

"Not tonight," Pauline said. "I have to write a letter to Roger."

"That won't take long," Curt said. "I'll even write it for you. Dear Roger. It's been nice, but I've just met the perfect man, and I'm madly in love. You and I can still be friends, though. Sincerely, Pauline." He jumped up and dunked the ball.

"Dreamer," Pauline said.

Lori picked up the ball and tossed it to Pauline. "Why don't you play for a little while?"

Pauline put up a lazy free throw that dropped

through the net. "Not with you two. I feel like Jack and the beanstalk." She headed for the main house. "I'll go say good-bye to Wanda. See you tomorrow."

Curt tossed Lori the ball. She dribbled it slowly, watching Pauline walk away. "She's a good player, even at her size. She made second team, all league, last year. But she doesn't know if she's going to play this fall. Says she has a lot of things going."

Curt took the ball from Lori and shot a left-handed hook. "I've heard that there was more to life than basketball, but I figured it was just a nasty rumor."

Lori caught the ball and dribbled to the free-throw line. She bounced the ball once and pumped it into the basket. Curt threw her the ball, and she sank another one. After making five in a row, she stepped away from the line. "I know when to quit." She passed the ball to Curt. "Are you really going out with her?"

"I don't know. I'm not sure I can squeeze into her little car." He flipped the ball into the basket, then tossed it to Lori.

"Look," Lori said, "I want to get something straight."

Curt stepped back. "This sounds serious, lady."

"I'm not kidding around," she said. "I just want you to know how things stand."

Curt sat down on the court. "Let's hear it."

"You're going to be a big hero at the high school this fall. You'll have all kinds of girls chasing after you."

"It's a tough life, but I'll try to put up with it."

"You'll be Joe Wheel on campus."

"Yeah, sure. Joe Wheel on his red-hot bicycle. Unless you'll give me a raise so I can buy a car."

"Will you quit interrupting me? I have something to say."

"I'm sorry. I thought we were having a talk. I didn't know you wanted to make a speech."

"You're doing it again."

"I'm finished." Curt clapped a hand over his mouth.

"All I'm saying is this: You'll have plenty of girls to choose from. I already know four or five who are dying to come out here and meet you." Curt bounced up and down, but he kept his hand over his mouth. "There are only two girls who are off limits—Pauline and me. That's while you're working here. After that, you can do anything you want." Lori turned away and shot the ball, missing the basket by three feet.

Curt bounced up and down, pointing at his mouth with his free hand.

"Go ahead," Lori said. "What do you want to say?"

Curt jerked his hand away from his mouth, took a huge breath, marched toward Lori, then whispered, "Okay."

Lori smiled and shook her head. "That's it?"

"No problem. Pauline's going steady, and she's too short anyway. And you? Forget it. You're cute, but you're too hard to get along with." Lori threw the ball at him and turned away. He wondered if he had gotten to her. "Besides, I don't care how good-looking she is, I won't get involved with anybody who has a better free-throw percentage than I do." He was almost sure Lori was blushing.

"Let's play ball," she said.

"Might as well," he told her. "All I can do is look at you anyway. The boss warned me about trying anything."

Lori stopped and looked him in the eye. "One more thing. I know that kind of talk is supposed to be really cool, but save it for Pauline or somebody. I don't like it."

He tossed her the ball. "I'm sorry I said you were cute."

"I'm serious," she shouted. "Cut it out."

"Let's play ball," he said. It would be a long time before he understood American girls. Maybe a lifetime.

July 10—7:30 A.M.

It was Tuesday, Lori's day off. When Curt came into the main house to start breakfast, Lori was sitting at the table. "Good morning, beautiful," he called out. She sneered and looked away. Curt grinned. He didn't want to push her too far, but he wasn't going to roll over and play dead either. "What's going on?" he asked. "You're supposed to sleep in today."

"I have an idea," she said. "Get yourself something to eat, and I'll tell you about it."

When Curt sat down with his corn flakes and juice, he looked across the table at her. She looked better than anybody had a right to that early in the morning, but he knew better than to say so. "What's the big brainstorm?"

"I need some help today. Are you willing to skip a couple of tours and find out a little about caves?"

Curt reached for the milk. "What's to know? I could walk through the whole tour with my eyes shut."

"Cathedral Caverns doesn't even count as a cave," Lori said. "It's something done for tourists. Look at it— blacktopped floor, cement stairs with handrails, electric lights, all the passageways widened and smoothed off. All we need is piped-in music."

"Why don't we raise the ceiling too? I'm turning into a hunchback."

"You know what they're doing at a lot of caves? They're operating spelunking expeditions. They take people into some of the undeveloped parts—let them crawl around and get dirty. And they charge a big price for it."

Curt looked up from his corn flakes. "People must be hard up for something to do."

"They're just looking for a little adventure. Where else can they go exploring these days?"

"Wait a minute," Curt said. "What does this have to do with me?"

"I've been thinking that we might be able to pick up some extra money by running a spelunking tour here. I want to check out some possibilities today, and I thought you might go along."

Curt stared at his bowl and kept eating.

"You don't have to go. I just thought you might be interested in seeing what a real cave is like."

He shrugged. "I'm not built for crawling around. Why don't you take Pauline?"

"It's nothing to worry about," she said. "I promise to take good care of you."

"Look," he said. "I'm not scared. The idea of crawling around and bumping my head just doesn't grab me."

Lori gave him a superior smile. "Oh, I know you're not scared. How could I ever imagine such a thing? I know it's more fun to run tours and mop the bathrooms than it is to go out and do something totally different."

Curt glared at her. "You think you've got me, don't you? If I don't go, it's because I'm chicken, right?"

Lori laughed. "Did I say the word *chicken*? Not me. I wonder what could have brought that into your mind."

Curt pushed his bowl away. "I get paid regular wages, right? This is your idea of how to spend your day off, not mine."

"You'll get paid," she said. "Just because I'm the nicest boss you'll ever have. Other people pay big bucks for a trip like this."

"I can't believe my luck," he muttered.

Curt led the first tour of the day. While he moved from room to room, he noticed dark crevices and small openings that he hadn't seen before. He wondered what dark twisting passageways lay beyond the light.

At ten o'clock he and Lori rode up the hill with Pauline and her group. Lori waited until the tourists had gone into the cave before she hauled a backpack out of the rear of the bus. "The last thing we need," she said, "is for some idiot to get the idea he can do this on his own. There are some undeveloped caves a few miles north of here. The owner has them all fenced off, but people keep breaking down the fence and going in." She shoved the pack toward Curt. "You carry this thing. It's my day off."

"Yes, boss."

They walked back down the road for a hundred yards, then headed uphill through the oaks and scrub brush. Lori led the way along a steep winding path. Curt was soon breathing hard, but he kept his mouth closed. He didn't want her laughing about his being out of shape.

She didn't look back once, and she didn't stop until they were standing on top of the ridge, looking at the blue bus far below. Curt slipped the backpack from his shoulders and sat down on the ground. He knew that she expected him to complain, so he smiled and said, "Nice view."

"See that?" Lori pointed toward a pile of cemented boulders. "That's the original opening that you tell people about six times a day. After Tanner drilled the tunnel, he had this closed off. It was dangerous, and he didn't want to get sued. One of the main trails in the cave led right to a dropoff, and the entranceway here was crumbling."

"Speaking of suing," Curt said, "if I get hurt, you think I could sue you?"

"No way. I'll claim that you talked me into it." She held her palm against her cheek and spoke in a squeaky voice. "I'm just a poor little girl. I had no idea what it would be like."

Curt laughed. "Lori, the helpless female. Good luck trying to sell that act."

She turned toward him. "Look, Curt, I'm going to show you something, and I want you to promise not to tell anybody."

"All right."

"I mean it. I want you to promise."

"What do you want me to do? Cross my heart and hope to die?"

"Just promise."

"I already did." He looked up at her and shook his head. "All right. You want it official?" He raised his right hand. "I solemnly promise not to tell whatever it is you're going to tell me, even if I'm tortured." He lowered his hand and added, "Unless it hurts."

"Come on." Lori strapped on the backpack and led the way down into a small ravine overgrown with pepperwood trees and elderberry bushes. They fought their way through the undergrowth for a while, then got to their knees and crawled beneath the branches. "It's grown up some since I was here," Lori said. She stopped beside a rotted log and let her pack slide to the ground.

"This had better be worth it," Curt said.

Lori pulled away part of the log, which crumbled in her hands. "Believe it or not, this is another entrance to the cave." As she pulled back more of the rotten wood, Curt could see a hole about the size of a basketball hoop. "Mom and I found this in the spring a couple of years ago. It was all plugged up, but water was coming out, so we knew something was there. We spent quite a while clearing it out—a bucketful at a time."

"Sounds like a barrel of laughs."

"It was fun. Like digging for treasure." She looked at him. "Only five people know about this—Mom, Wanda, Pauline, you, and me. And Wanda's never been up here."

"What about Pauline?"

"She came with me a couple of times. She didn't like it much."

"I always thought that girl had good sense."

Lori opened the backpack and brought out two orange hardhats with sealed beam lights on the visors. "I hope this one is big enough for you." She shoved a hat toward him. "You clip the battery pack on the back of your belt. That way, it won't get caught on something." Lori put on her hat, then helped him adjust the chinstrap on his.

"I don't know what to do," he said.

"All you have to do is crawl. Just keep your head up and your bottom down. Sometimes you'll be on your hands and knees, and sometimes you'll have to do it snake style—just kind of squiggle forward. Don't worry, and don't get in a rush. It'll be fun."

"I'll bet."

She handed him the water bottle. "Besides, it's a lot cooler in there." She dropped to her knees. "Just follow me. It's not too far, but it'll seem like a long way. If you get tired, stop and rest for a second. You know where your light switch is, right?"

Curt reached behind his back and flicked the switch up and down.

"If the light gets shut off accidentally, don't worry. Just reach back there and turn it on again." She looked up at him. "Are you ready?"

"No," he said.

"No use waiting around." She put her head into the hole and stretched out on the ground.

"This is crazy," Curt said aloud, watching Lori's feet disappear. He lay down on his stomach and peered into the hole. The light from his helmet shone on the soles of Lori's shoes. He sighed and crawled forward into the cool passageway.

Once he had started, Curt was surprised at how well he could see with just the single light. The only problem was that he could only see straight in front of him. If he wanted to look down or to the side, he had to move his head that way.

The passageway was never the same size for long. With each turn it expanded or shrank. Curt couldn't see any pattern in the changes, although he didn't think about it long. He just kept crawling along, banging his hardhat and sometimes his backbone on the rock above him. At first the floor of the passageway was mostly sand. Then it became smooth rock, with an occasional rounded mound sticking up. Then it was sand again. Curt was sure that water must run through there in the wet seasons.

Lori's feet had disappeared. She was probably trying

to outrun him—just to show him. He crawled faster, hoping to catch her again, but he soon had to stop and catch his breath.

Once he quit moving, nightmarish ideas came pouring over him. What if there was an earthquake? What if he took a wrong passage? What if he got stuck somewhere? Were there bats in here? Or snakes? Was there enough oxygen? He jerked up, banging his head, and started forward, faster than before.

He squeezed through a narrow opening, then pulled himself up what would have been a foot-high waterfall. He slid forward and found himself looking into another light.

The light went out, and Lori came crawling toward him. "Isn't this neat?" she said, stopping with her head a foot from his. Curt wanted to reach out and touch her.

"It's great." He didn't sound very convincing, even to himself.

"I love the colors here."

Curt glanced around at the yellowish rock, laced with reds and greens. It was the first time he had thought about color. "How'd you get turned around?"

"There's a fork right up here. The passage on the left only goes a few feet before it gets too small, but it makes a good turnaround. Are you doing okay?"

"If I was paying for this, I'd want my money back."

Lori laughed and began scooting backward. "It's a little harder in reverse."

"How much farther?" Curt asked.

"Just a little way. There's a big room up ahead."

"Good. I'm dying to stand up and stretch."

"You'll be able to stand up in some places," she said, "but I'm not sure about stretching."

"I'll settle for standing up." He stayed close to her while she wriggled backward.

"All right," she said. "Hold it a second. Here's where I make the turn." He watched her move farther away. Then her light came on, and she rolled onto her side. A minute later he was following her shoes again.

Curt tried to look at the colors and the shapes, but soon he was working mechanically again. It took all of his energy and attention to keep moving forward.

The passage grew wider, and he moved up onto his hands and knees. Each time he jammed a knee down on a rock, he decided that next time he would bring kneepads. Except that there wouldn't be a next time.

When he crawled into the room, he didn't bother to stand up. He just stretched out on a flat spot and rolled onto his back. The battery pack dug into his spine. He thought about taking off the pack but rolled over onto his side instead.

Lori came over and sat down near his head. "How you doing?"

"I'm not built right for this crawling business."

"We'll rest awhile. Then I want to check out some of the passages here. They go heading off in all directions."

"Mmhh." Curt didn't bother to look.

"The secret to spelunking is to check everything. You keep going into holes, and once in a while you find something. That's how they found the Cathedral Room. They kept poking around, and they found a way down, and they ended up at the top of the room. Can you imagine what that would have been like—to be the first person to see that?"

"Mmhh."

Soon Lori was ready to go. "I want to check out the

area over here to the right. I was thinking that we could bring in spelunkers and then let them look into some of the openings."

Curt stood up and followed her over the rocks, keeping his head low. Lori stopped at a point where the floor of the room disappeared under a rock wall. She handed Curt a notebook. "You're the secretary." She took a piece of green chalk from her pocket and picked up a big stone. She chalked L-1 on the stone and set it beside the opening. "You have to have some kind of system, or you'll end up going into the same places over and over." She dropped down onto her stomach.

"What do I do?" Curt asked her.

"Just wait here. I may yell out some stuff for you to write down. Don't worry if you have trouble hearing me. Sound doesn't carry very well in a cave." She wriggled under the overhang. "I'll see you soon."

After she was gone, Curt wondered what he would do if she didn't come back. Was he supposed to go in after her? Or go for help? He thought he could find his way back to the place where they came in, but he wasn't really sure of that. He turned his head from side to side, watching his light travel over the walls and the rocks. She'd better come back.

He saw her light a minute before her head popped out. "Write this down. L-1—wedge-shaped room, goes thirty feet back, soda straws on the ceiling, easy entry." She looked up at Curt. "You want a quick tour?"

"Save it for the paying customers."

Lori checked out and marked six more possibilities. Two of them didn't amount to anything. Another dead-ended after ten feet, and she had to crawl out backward. "That gives us four side trips," she said. "Do you think that's enough for a good tour?"

"Listen," Curt said, "by that time they'll be begging you to get them out of here."

Lori took the notebook and stuffed it into a pocket. "While we're here, I want you to see the way the first people got to the Cathedral Room."

"Right now the only thing I want to see is daylight," he said, but he followed her into a low section of the room.

Early explorers had marked the passageway with black from their carbide lamps, and somebody later on had painted a red X above the opening. Lori led the way along the twisting passage, first doing a duck walk, then dropping to her hands and knees when the passageway shrank.

"Wait a minute," Curt said. "I've had all the crawling I need."

"Quit moaning," Lori said. "It's just a little ways."

He thought about stopping right there, but he knew what she'd say. Never again, though. Once he was out of here, he'd never be back.

When the passage grew too narrow for him to crawl on his hands and knees, he couldn't keep up with her. The soles of her boots disappeared around a bend, and he was alone. He was sure she was leaving him on purpose. For Lori, this was another game. And this time she was winning.

For a while he crawled on his knees and forearms, his body flattened out so that he wouldn't scrape his backbone. He decided to turn around and head back at the first wide spot.

But there were no wide spots. The passageway grew even smaller and slanted upward. Curt couldn't get up on his knees at all, so he had to develop a new crawl. He lay with his chest on his forearms, his fists on either side of his neck. He could then use his forearms to scoot himself forward. He didn't break any speed records, but he kept moving.

Lori's light shone in his face. "Just a little more," she called.

"I don't fit," he called back. He scooted toward her, his body scraping the walls on both sides.

"Take it easy when you get out here," Lori said. "We don't have much room."

Curt pulled himself a few feet closer, moving beyond the walls. The rock ceiling was still just above him.

"Hold onto this." She grabbed his fingers and placed them on an iron ring big enough for his hand to fit through. His fingers wrapped around the cold metal. "Now you can move your legs out the other way."

Curt looked ahead and saw his light reflect off a rock wall. "What is this?"

"End of the line," Lori said. "There's a dropoff here." She reached her foot over the edge. "From here they used ropes to get down. That's what the ring is for."

Curt stretched out on the ledge, keeping a solid grip on the ring.

"Turn off your light," Lori said.

"What for?"

"I want to show you something."

"I don't want to see it." But he reached back and flipped off his light. He shuddered at the darkness. The rock beneath him seemed to be moving. He reached out and grabbed the ring with his other hand.

"See that glow way off to the left?" Lori said. "That's the lights from the Cathedral Room."

Now that he had both hands on the ring, Curt felt steady enough to look around. "Have you ever gone down from here?" he asked after a minute.

"Mom and I did it once. We found a whole bunch of little rooms off to the sides. That might make an even better spelunking area than the one up here. We could go up a ladder from the Cathedral Room and then explore that area."

"That'd be some ladder," Curt said, reaching for his battery pack. He felt himself relax when the light flashed on.

"You sound like a guy who's had enough caving for one day," Lori said.

Curt figured he'd had enough caving for one lifetime, but he didn't say so.

Lori turned on her light and crawled into the opening. Curt followed right behind. Soon he was inching down the incline, feeling as if he were doing a dive. Lori's feet were already out of sight.

Just beyond his helmet was an opening not much bigger than his head. He could hardly believe he'd made it past there. Stretching his arms straight out, he eased himself through, one shoulder at a time. The walls scraped his sides.

Pulling himself forward, he felt a sharp tug at his waist. He tried to jerk loose, but he couldn't get any momentum. He ran his hands over the walls and floor in front of him, searching for something to hold on to. He dug his fingers into a crack and tried to pull forward. Again and again he grasped the crack and pulled until his fingers slipped. But he didn't move.

He pushed up against one wall as hard as he could, trying to get enough room to bring his hand back. He kept trying it long after he knew that it was impossible.

"Lori," he called. "Lori." He listened for a minute, hearing nothing.

"Help!" he screamed, his hat banging against the ceiling. "I'm caught! Help! Help! Help!"

Curt kept screaming that one word until he couldn't get his breath. Then his face smacked the ground, and he lay still and sucked in air, his pulse hammering in his head. It was stupid to yell that way. He couldn't have heard Lori if she had answered him.

When his breathing slowed a little, he yelled, "Help" once, then waited. He was about to yell again when Lori's boots appeared at the bottom of the incline. "Lori," he screamed, "I'm stuck."

Lori's voice sounded miles away. "Try to back up."

Curt braced his arms against the walls and pushed. Nothing happened. He tried to edge one foot backward, but he felt the same tug at his waist. He arched his back until he could feel the rock through his shirt. He wiggled back and forth, smiling when he actually moved. He braced his arms and arched his back once more.

His light went out. "My light!" he yelled. "My light! Lori, my light's out, and I'm stuck!"

When he stopped yelling, Lori called, "Can you hear me?"

"Barely."

"I have to go ahead until I can turn around. Don't worry. I'll get you loose. Go ahead and yell if you want to. It might make you feel better."

Curt lay and gritted his teeth. She sounded so smug and sure of herself. Well, he wasn't about to yell. He wouldn't give her the satisfaction. He dug his fingers into the crack and tried to pull himself forward. When that didn't work, he arched his back and flattened his palms against the rock. He pushed backward with all his strength.

His hands slid forward on the rough rock, tearing the skin on his palms. "You moron!" he screamed. "I didn't want to come here. I didn't want any part of this! This whole thing's your stupid fault. I hate you. I hate everything about you. I . . . HATE . . . YOU." He let his head sag against the cool floor of the passageway. She was right. Yelling did help—a little.

He started to squirm again when he saw a faint glow in front of him. He didn't want her to think he wasn't trying. He pushed and yanked while the light grew brighter. Then the light was in his eyes as Lori scooted up the incline toward him.

She reached out and put a hand on his cheek. He realized that his cheek was damp, but he couldn't remember crying. "You didn't need this," she said quietly.

"I'm stuck," he moaned.

Lori kept rubbing his cheek. "Well, we're going to get you unstuck. It's rough when it happens. I'm glad you're doing all right. I was afraid you'd be a basket case."

Curt opened his mouth, then closed it to cut off a sob.

She took his face in her hands and gave it a squeeze. "You're doing fine." She tapped his cheeks. "Now let's see about getting you out of here. Where are you caught?"

"My belt, I think."

"Top or bottom?"

"Right behind my back. I tried to move backwards, but I can't."

Lori scooted away from him and slipped off her hat. "You hold this off to the side and keep the light pointed toward you," she said. "I'm going to try to reach back there." She inched forward, slipping her hand between his shoulder blades. "This is going to get a little cozy."

"I'm not complaining," he said.

Soon they were cheek to cheek while her hand pulled at his belt. "It's hooked over something sticking out," Lori said through clenched teeth. "I can't get enough slack to get it off." Curt felt her body relax. Her cheek sagged against his chin. "I want to try to scoot you backwards. When I say, 'Three,' shove back with everything you have, and I'll push on you."

Curt set her hat down carefully and shoved his hands against the rock walls. His palms burned. "I'm ready."

Lori stiffened and placed a hand against his shoulder. "One. Two. Three."

Feeling Lori shove, Curt pushed backward with all his strength. He knew that he was moving because his arms extended an inch or two.

"Hold it right there," Lori shouted. "I think I can do it now." Curt felt her hand moving over his back. "Okay, I think you're clear. But don't do anything until I get out of the way."

Lori scooted backward and put on her hat. "Now come forward. Are you clear?"

Curt eased himself toward her, keeping his stomach flat on the ground. "I'm loose," he shouted. "Oh, man, I'm free."

"Good." She reached out and touched his cheek again. "Now I get to back out of here." She wriggled away from him, the light on her hat bobbing up and down. Curt kept his eyes on the ground in front of him so that the light wouldn't blind him.

At the first place where the cave widened, Curt reached back and flipped on his own light. "You don't need that right now," Lori said. "It just gets in my eyes." He flipped off the light, glad to know that it worked.

When the passageway widened a little more, Lori managed to turn around. Curt turned on his light and stayed right on her heels until they were back in the big room.

Curt sat down hard, and Lori turned toward him. "How are you doing?"

"I'm okay," he said. "I guess I made an idiot of myself back there."

"Forget it." Then she looked his way and smiled. "Too bad I didn't have a tape recorder, though. I could play it back once in a while when you needed it."

Curt felt his cheeks burn, but he managed to keep his mouth closed. He turned away and stretched out on the ground. By then, he was ready for her. "You planned the whole thing. You just wanted an excuse to get your hands on my body."

"You're right," she said, squatting down beside him. "But it wasn't worth it. You're fat and flabby." She looked at him, her light flashing into his eyes. "Actually, you did great. You didn't panic at all."

"Maybe a little." He reached out and put his hand on hers. "Hey, Lori, thanks for your help."

"Sure, Curt," she said quietly. Then she pulled away from him and stood up. "We'd better get going."

"You don't have to run away," he said. "I wasn't making a move on you. I was just being friendly."

Lori didn't look at him. "Don't flatter yourself. I'm not running away. I just figured we'd better get back before Pauline and Wanda get mad and go on strike."

"Sure." Curt stood up and followed her. *Had* he been making a move?

5

July 16—6:00 P.M.

Curt put down the telephone and said, "Deputies on the way. Sheriff 'll be here in a few minutes."

Lori dug in a drawer and brought out a handful of pencils. "You'd better tell Wanda." She grabbed a stack of memo pads from the stationery rack and started for the door. "I'll get those people to write down everything they can remember."

Curt flipped on the intercom, hit the switch for the main house, and said, "Wanda, can you come over here right away?"

While he waited for Wanda, he read through the note again. It covered two pages of typing paper—block letters done in blue ballpoint ink:

WE, THE BROTHERHOOD OF NEW FREEDOM, HAVE TAKEN PAULINE THOMAS AS A PRISONER OF WAR. SHE WILL NOT BE HARMED AS LONG AS OUR ORDERS ARE FOLLOWED EXACTLY.

WE NEED THE FOLLOWING SUPPLIES: 15 CANS OF PEACHES OR PEARS, 15 CANS OF BEANS OR SPAGHETTI, 100 BOTTLES OF PERRIER, 15 CANS OF UNFLAVORED ICED TEA, 3 SLEEPING BAGS, 3 AIR MATTRESSES, A PROPANE STOVE WITH FUEL, A CAN OPENER, PLASTIC FORKS AND SPOONS IN UNOPENED

BOXES. THESE SUPPLIES ARE TO BE BROUGHT UP ON THE BUS AND LEFT OUTSIDE THE DOOR OF THE CAVE WITHIN TWO HOURS.

PAULINE THOMAS WILL BE FREED UNHARMED IF THE FOLLOWING STEPS ARE TAKEN: THE PRICE FOR HER RELEASE IS FIVE HUNDRED THOUSAND DOL-LARS, TO BE PAID IN USED BILLS, FIFTY DOLLARS AND SMALLER. TWO HUNDRED AND FIFTY THOUSAND DOLLARS IS TO BE PLACED OUTSIDE THE CAVE DOOR BY FIVE O'CLOCK TOMORROW AFTERNOON. THAT MONEY WILL BE EXAMINED CAREFULLY TO BE SURE IT IS UNMARKED. AT TEN O'CLOCK THE FOLLOWING MORNING, THE REST OF THE MONEY IS TO BE LEFT OUTSIDE THE CAVE DOOR. AT ELEVEN O'CLOCK A TELEVISION CREW OF NO MORE THAN THREE PER-SONS SHOULD BE OUTSIDE THE CAVE DOOR. WE WILL PRESENT A STATEMENT AT THAT TIME.

AT TWELVE O'CLOCK THE OLD WOMAN WHO WORKS AT THE CAVE WILL BRING THE BUS TO ITS PARKING PLACE BESIDE THE CAVE STEPS. WE WILL LEAVE THE CAVE AND RIDE WITH HER TO THE PARK-ING LOT, WHERE MR. THOMAS'S CHAUFFEUR WILL HAVE MR. THOMAS'S CADILLAC LIMOUSINE WAITING. HE WILL DRIVE US TO THE BARKER MILLS AIRPORT, WHERE MR. THOMAS'S PERSONAL JET IS TO BE WAIT-ING ON THE RUNWAY WITH FULL TANKS. GATES MUST BE OPEN SO THAT WE CAN DRIVE ONTO THE RUN-WAY. NO PILOT WILL BE NEEDED.

OUR CAUSE IS JUST, AND WE ARE WILLING TO DIE FOR IT. THE CAVE DOOR IS WIRED WITH EXPLOSIVES. ANY ATTEMPT TO ENTER BY FORCE WILL RESULT IN TRAGEDY. WE HAVE NO WISH TO HARM PAULINE THOMAS, BUT HER DEATH IS NO MORE IMPORTANT THAN THE DEATH OF ANY OF THE THOUSANDS OF

OUR BROTHERS AND SISTERS WHO DIE OF STARVA-
TION EACH YEAR.

Curt set the note on the counter. He felt more hope-
ful, although he wasn't sure why. Maybe because the
note was so well organized. At least they weren't dealing with psychos. But who except a psycho would do
something like this?

Wanda came through the back door. "What's the
matter, Curtis?"

"Pauline is being held in the cave by kidnappers," he
said, realizing how crazy that sounded.

Wanda closed her eyes, muttering to herself while
Curt told her about the note. She staggered toward the
counter like a sleepwalker. "I knew it," she said. "I
knew those two weren't right, and I was too stupid to do
anything about it."

"What are you talking about?"

"A guy in a baseball cap and sunglasses came in about
five minutes before the tour started. He had a big bushy
beard that didn't look real, and he was wearing a black
sweatshirt. A hundred degrees out there, and he had on
a sweatshirt. Never said a word. Just held up two fingers
and laid down the money. I asked him something, but
he just nodded his head and went right back outside."
She looked at Curt. "I'm so stupid, Curtis."

"Come on. How could you know?"

"It didn't take a genius. I was bothered enough to go
over to the window and take another look at him. The
guy with him had on a sweatshirt too. And a beard.
They just looked wrong, but I didn't do anything. And I
should have." Wanda turned away from him, her head
down. "Lord, I hope she's all right."

The first deputies came inside the store long enough

to look at the note, then headed for the bus. A minute
later Lori came back inside. "They didn't appreciate
my help," she said.

"Did you find out anything?" Curt asked her.

"Not much. Two kidnappers—both fat, one kind of
tall, the other medium. Beards and sunglasses. As far as
I can tell, they said four words. After everybody was in
the Cathedral Room, they moved back by the entrance
and yelled, 'Stop.' One of them had a pistol, and the
other had a hand grenade. Then one of them said, 'Out,'
and pointed at the cave entrance. They stood back and
let everybody go by except Pauline. When she came
up, they said, 'Not you.' The one with the pistol gave
the note to one of the women. Didn't say anything. Just
gave her the note." Lori shook her head. "Not much
help."

"Wanda figures the beards are fake," Curt said. "And
anybody can stuff a pillow in his shirt."

Wanda turned to face them. Her eyes were red, and
her cheeks were flushed. "Oh, honey, I'm so scared."

Lori rushed toward her. "Me too, Wanda. It just
hasn't hit me yet." She grabbed Wanda and pulled her
close.

Feeling a lump in his throat, Curt walked to the front
window. Two more patrol cars drove into the parking
lot. A short, barrel-chested man climbed out of the second car and looked around. One of the deputies trotted
toward him, carrying the note. "I think the sheriff's
here," Curt said.

The sheriff moved into the shade to read the note.
After several minutes he waved for a deputy to follow
him and came into the store. "How you doing, Curtis?"
he said. "I'm Walt Quinlan." He crunched Curt's hand.
"Hello, Wanda." He waved in her direction.

Lori hurried forward. "Sheriff, I'm Lori Matthews. I'm running the cave this summer."

Sheriff Quinlan took her hand. "Hi, Lori. I've met your mother a few times." He pointed toward the deputy by the door. "That's Jerry. We need your phone and a phone book. We've got a few supplies to order here."

Lori took the book out of the drawer, and Quinlan handed it to the deputy. "I've already located Ray Thomas. He was in San Luis Obispo, but he'll be here in a couple of hours. In the meantime we'll keep everything nice and easy."

"Have you heard anything?" Lori asked.

"I don't know a thing you don't." He looked at the note. "I never in my life heard of the Brotherhood of New Freedom. But right now we're going to do our best to keep the Brotherhood happy as clams." He handed Jerry the note. "Looks like those boys are worried about getting poisoned. Want everything in cans. Well, we'll do it their way." He looked toward Wanda. "Do they have any cake or cookies that come in sealed cans?"

"I think so," Wanda said.

"Tell them to check," Quinlan told Jerry. "Tell them to throw in some canned pudding. Anything sweet in a can. And twice as much canned stuff as they ordered. And three or four can openers. And get them a portable toilet and some paper, will you?" He looked over at Lori. "We want everything just right for those people. Do you have some magazines and books around here? We'll throw in a few. Help those boys pass the time."

While Jerry telephoned, Quinlan took the three of them aside. "This a high-class outfit," he said. "They're going to be washing their faces in Perrier." He looked at each of them. "I'll have time to talk to you folks later on. Right now I need to see the people on the bus. But first, do any of you know anything that might help us?"

"I think the beards are fake," Wanda said. "One of them is a little over six feet, and the other's about five-nine. That's not much, I know."

Quinlan shrugged. "Doesn't matter. We'll see 'em on TV soon enough." He headed out the door.

Curt, Lori, and Wanda sat in a half circle by the window, saying nothing. One by one the tourists came off the bus and headed across the parking lot for their cars.

"I wonder if any of them wanted their money back," Lori said.

A deputy opened the door and said that the sheriff wanted to see them. They went outside to the parking lot where Quinlan was waving good-bye to a family in a station wagon. "Okay," he said, "that was the last bunch. Which one of these cars don't you recognize?"

They glanced around quickly. "They're all ours," Lori said. "The pickup and the Chevy belong to Mom, and the Plymouth is Wanda's."

"And that's Pauline's Corvette," Curt added.

Quinlan glanced around. "Is there anywhere else to park a car around here?" They all shook their heads. "Then we'd better get the boys looking for a car up the road. Why don't you people go get something to eat? I'll talk to you in a while."

They went inside and heated some packaged sandwiches in the snack bar microwave. Curt ate his without tasting it, then ate the one Wanda shoved his way.

Quinlan came in and ate a sandwich while he questioned them about the work schedule and the cave routine. "Those boys knew what they were doing," he said finally. "They wanted the last bunch of the day— after the other group was gone."

A deputy opened the door and said, "Nothing."

"We've searched the whole area," Quinlan said. "No car." He shook his head. "They must have had somebody drop them off. I can't believe they took a taxi, but we'll check just the same."

"I'd have seen a taxi pull up," Wanda said.

Quinlan looked around. "We're keeping the reporters out on the highway until the supplies get delivered. Then we'll have to let 'em in, I guess. I think I'd better do the talking, though." He ran the back of his hand across his forehead. "You see, we don't want to tell everything. With a thing like this, we'll get a bunch of fruitcakes calling in. We need to hold back some of the details so if the real people call us, we'll know it's them."

"Why let the reporters in at all?" Wanda said. "We don't need 'em around here."

Quinlan smiled. "Those people gotta make a living too. I'll give 'em enough to keep everybody happy. If they ask you anything, just tell 'em to ask me."

The supplies arrived in a white van. While the deputies loaded them onto the bus, Quinlan spoke to Curt. "Do you mind driving the bus up there? I know what that road's like, and I'd rather have somebody driving who's used to it."

"Sure," Curt said, glad to have something to do.

On the way uphill Curt had his cave spiel running through his mind. ("The first white settlers to enter the cave were . . .") The deputies sat in the seats directly behind his and stared straight ahead. He wondered if the narrow road was bothering them.

When he reached the turnaround area and started backing into the loading zone, one of the deputies said, "You stay in the bus. We'll carry the supplies."

After the first trip up the sixty-two steps, though, the deputy suggested that Curt might help them. "You can take a look around up there. See if anything looks different."

Nothing looked different. The cave door was shut tight, as usual. But the deputies let him make a second and third trip just the same.

When he got back to the store, nothing was different there either. Lori and Wanda were sitting by the window. Sheriff Quinlan was stirring a cup of coffee while he talked on the phone.

When Quinlan finished, he wandered over toward them. "Better rest while you can. Mr. Thomas will be here pretty soon, and then we'll let the reporters in. I'm going to send some of my boys home now. I don't think anything's going to happen tonight." He sipped his coffee. "One thing's sure, the boys from the Brotherhood aren't going anywhere."

Lori glanced at Curt, then said, "Sheriff, it probably isn't important, but there *is* another way in and out of the cave."

Quinlan reached out and grabbed her shoulder. "What?"

"It's not like that," Lori said. She went on and told him about the opening that she and her mother had found.

"But somebody could get out that way?" Quinlan asked when she was finished.

"Only if they'd gone in there ahead of time and put ropes in place."

Quinlan thought for a minute. "Well, I guess we'd better check it out."

July 16—9:30 P.M.

Curt set down his backpack and watched Lori drag the rotten log away from the opening. "This is the place," she called to the deputies—a younger man named Robbie and a heavyset man named Mike.

"It's about time," Robbie said, smashing his way into the clearing. "Where is it?"

Curt pointed to the opening. Robbie knelt down and shone his light around. "You really went inside here?"

"We both did," Lori said. "Last week." She set her flashlight on a rock so that it lit up the area. Then she opened the backpack and took out a hardhat.

"I don't think we'll be needing those," Robbie said.

Lori kept dragging things out of the pack. "Sheriff Quinlan said for us to go in and see if they've put in ropes."

"Quin hadn't seen the size of that rabbit hole. I don't think there's any danger of fat kidnappers climbing out of there."

"But he said—" Lori began.

"Let's be sensible," Robbie said. "You two were up here last week. You put that log over the hole. Does it look like anybody moved it?"

"No," Curt said.

"What about you, miss? Do you think it's been moved?"

"I don't know," Lori said. "But the sheriff said—"

"I think we've seen all we need to see, miss. Nobody knows about this entrance, and nobody in his right mind would crawl into it." He turned away and shouted, "Don't bother coming down, Mike. We're on our way out."

"Suits me," Mike called from above.

"You don't have to go in," Lori said. "I'll go in by myself."

Robbie checked his watch. "We'd better get back." He knelt beside Lori and shoved the hats back into the pack. Then he slid his arms through the shoulder straps and stood up. "Let's see if we can get out of here faster than we got in."

Lori sat down on the ground. "I'm not going."

Robbie reached over and grabbed Lori's flashlight off the rock. "Suit yourself, miss. But it's going to be pretty dark up here." He turned and started through the brush.

"Give that back," Lori shouted, jumping to her feet.

"Come on, miss," Robbie said, waving her forward with the light. "Lead the way out of here."

Lori didn't say a word on the way back. Mike, who was waiting at the top of the hill, laughed about who would draw hole-watching duty. "After the money's delivered, Quin'll probably send somebody up here just to be sure. But it'll be the guy who's on the top of his buzzard bait list. Is that you, Robbie? You gonna get buzzard bait duty?"

"Not me," Robbie said. "I'm not even close. It'll be Hartman or you."

"You got it all wrong," Mike said. "Quin chews on me now and then, but he knows I'm okay."

"For buzzard bait duty," Robbie said.

When they reached the bus garage, Mike stopped them. "You go see Quin," he told Robbie. "See what he wants us to do."

Curt took off the backpack that Robbie had given him halfway down the hill. "What's the matter?"

"Orders," Mike said.

Lori snorted. "I didn't see anybody jumping to follow orders up there."

Quinlan came out of the main house and ambled in their direction. "I'll bet you folks are a little beat."

"It's ridiculous," Lori said. "They wouldn't even go in there to have a look."

Quinlan nodded. "I heard all about it. Now I want you two to gather up some clothes and things. Lori, you'll take the Chevrolet and go stay with your friend Janet. Wanda's already called her. And Curtis, you'll stay with your coach. Lori can drop you on her way. We'll telephone you if we need you."

"I'm in charge of the place here," Lori said. "I can't just—"

"Wanda'll be here."

Lori took a breath and let it go. "So you're going to ship us out."

"I think things will work better this way. We're going to have a lot of people around here. It looks like Curtis is going to have a millionaire sleeping in his bed tonight."

"You don't have any right," Lori started, then turned away.

"Get your stuff together," Quinlan said. "Once you

and Curt have your things in the car, I'll take you into the store. The television people already have their story, but they want to get your pictures. I've told 'em you won't be answering any questions."

Lori snorted and said to Curt, "You know what this is all about, don't you? He doesn't trust us around the reporters."

Quinlan shrugged. "The only thing that matters right now is that little girl up in the cave."

Curt threw some clothes in a duffel bag, then waited by the Chevrolet for fifteen minutes before Lori finally showed up. A deputy was carrying her suitcase.

Quinlan met them in front of the store and led them inside. When the camera lights came on, Curt realized that he hadn't combed his hair. "Look toward me," one of the cameramen called out. Curt kept his eyes straight ahead. What did they expect him to do—smile and say, "Hi, Mom," the way all the athletes on television did?

"Is this the boy who called the sheriff?" somebody asked.

"How do you feel right now?" a woman by the cash register asked in a soft voice.

"Mad," Lori burst out.

"That'll be all," Quinlan said quickly. He led them out the front door and across the parking lot to the Chevrolet. One cameraman followed along behind them, his lights throwing their shadows ahead of them. Curt climbed into the car to get away.

Quinlan opened the door on the driver's side. "If anything happens tonight, I'll have somebody call you," he told Lori. "But nothing will. Now, nobody knows where you're staying, but if a reporter finds you, don't talk to him. When this is all over and that little girl is safe, then you can talk all you want."

Lori slid behind the steering wheel. "Your men wouldn't even go in the cave. For all you know, the kidnappers may be planning to get out that way."

"Don't worry. We'll be covering all the bases. You just get some sleep." Quinlan slammed the door and waved them off.

Lori started the engine and yanked the gearshift into reverse. "They're morons." The Chevrolet shot backwards. Lori hit the brake hard, shifted gears, and stamped on the accelerator.

Once the car shot out of the parking lot, Lori slowed down. "They're supposed to know what they're doing, right? These are the pros. And they won't even go into the cave and take a look."

"I guess they figured—"

"They're absolute morons," Lori broke in. "I went into my bedroom just now, locked the door, and went out the window. I was all over the place. Gone about twenty minutes. Do you think any of those pros knew I was gone? I could have been blowing up the place, and they wouldn't have known the difference."

"What *were* you doing?"

"Putting some stuff together. If they won't go in there and look, I'll go by myself." She hit the brake, throwing Curt toward the windshield.

"What's the matter?"

"You take the car and go on into town. When you get to Coach Franks's place, call Janet. Her last name is Hurley. Look up George Hurley in the phone book. Tell her I won't be coming."

"Wait a minute, Lori."

"Do that much for me, will you? I'll check the cave

and be back down before anybody knows I'm gone."
She opened the door and looked over at Curt. "Please.
I've got to do something."
"I'll go up there with you," he said.
"But you've got to—"
"We'll make two phone calls."
Lori put a hand on his arm. "Are you sure?"
"I wouldn't sleep anyway."
Lori slammed the door and put the car into gear.
"Then let's do it."

A patrol car was parked across the entrance to the
cave turnoff. A bored-looking deputy waved as they
squeezed past.

After making their calls from a pay phone two miles
down the road, they drove back and hid the car in a
stand of trees about two hundred yards from the turnoff. They skirted around the patrol car, then followed
the driveway until they could see the lights from the
store.

They crept through the trees to the cave road. Curt
waited there while Lori went to get her backpack. "You
see?" she whispered when she came back. "A whole
army of terrorists could sneak in while those people are
drinking coffee and deciding what to do. I'll bet we
could sneak right past the ones guarding the cave entrance too."

"What good would that do?"

"I'm just making a point," she said. "Let's go."

When they reached the opening again, Lori set her
flashlight on a rock and dug into the backpack. "You
have the feeling you've been here before?" she said.

Curt sat down on the ground. "It's been a long day."

Lori pulled the orange hardhats from her pack, then

tossed Curt a sweatshirt. "You'd better put this on. It's a little small, but it'll be okay."

"You figured I'd come, didn't you?"

"I didn't know what you'd do."

"You didn't have the slightest idea, but you packed a hat and a sweatshirt for me just in case."

"I also brought you a candy bar." She tossed it into his lap. "Eat it and shut up."

Curt tore off the wrapper. "Every once in a while you do something smart."

"Just rest a minute," Lori said. "I want to put fresh batteries in our packs."

"Two more good ideas. You're on a roll." Curt leaned back against a rock and closed his eyes.

The next thing he knew, Lori was poking him. "I never saw anybody go to sleep so fast in my life," she said.

He stretched out his arms and yawned. "You want to see me do it again?"

"Time to go," she said, handing him his hat and battery pack.

Curt clipped the pack to his belt, shivering when he felt the pull on his waist. He settled his hat on his head and flipped on his light. Lori dropped to her knees and moved toward the opening. In her left hand was a coil of rope, wrapped in a tight figure eight. "What's the rope for?"

"It may come in handy." Her head disappeared into the opening.

Curt scooted forward. This time he'd keep her in sight.

For a while he counted movements forward, as if he were climbing stairs. Snatches of old songs flashed into his mind, but he kept counting. It drove the other thoughts away.

When he lost sight of Lori, he scrambled ahead furiously until her boots came into sight again. By then he had lost count.

There was no reason to panic. He could see Lori's boots, and he had been through this passage before. "Cool and easy," he whispered, crawling forward. "Cool and easy, cool and easy." A train engine rhythm ran in his mind, and he moved with each syllable.

They rested for a minute in the big room, then made their way across to the passage marked with the red *X*. "We're making good time," Lori said.

"I still don't know why anybody'd pay to do this."

In the next passage he counted movements again until he passed four hundred. When they reached the section where he had to crawl upward, he kept looking for the spot where he had been stuck. "Cool and easy," he whispered. "Cool and easy." Twice he thought he recognized the place, and each time he felt his stomach contract.

Then Lori's light was in his face, and she was guiding his hand to the ring. "Here we are," she whispered.

Curt lay down on the ledge. "No escape ropes here, right? So we did all this work for nothing."

"At least we know."

Hearing her moving around, Curt raised his head. "What's the hurry?" She was uncoiling her rope. "What are you doing?"

"I want to go down and take a look."

"You're crazy."

"It'll only take a few minutes."

Curt sat up, banging his head on the rock. "You

planned this all along, didn't you? That's why you brought the rope."

"I just thought—"

"Thanks for telling me, Lori."

Lori tied one end of the rope to the ring, then fed the rest of the coil over the edge. "I'm sorry," she said.

"Don't give me that. You had it all planned out."

"I was thinking about Pauline, all right?" She reached over the edge and grasped the rope in both hands. "Getting started is the tricky part." She slipped one leg off the ledge, then began to slide, digging her toe into the rock to slow herself.

Curt set his hat aside, then grabbed the ring and leaned over the edge to watch her go down the rope. When she reached the bottom, she stepped away and waved. She wasn't as far down as he'd expected.

Trying to get comfortable, Curt finally ended up with his feet back in the passage. That way he could stretch out almost straight. Lori's light bounced along, moving slowly toward the glow he could see to his left. Then her light was gone.

After waiting a long time, Curt flipped on his light and checked his watch. He turned off the light and tried to wait five minutes. When he was sure five minutes had passed, he counted to a hundred, then turned on the light. Four minutes had gone by. The next time he waited six minutes. He was on the third try when he spotted Lori's light.

When she started up the rope, he moved around and braced his legs. When her hand reached up for the ring, he grabbed her wrist and helped her onto the ledge. She caught her breath for a second, grinning at him and bobbing her head up and down. Then she whispered, "I saw her."

"Pauline?"

Lori's head bobbed up and down again. "She's all alone in the Cathedral Room."

"Is she all right?"

"I think so. She's blindfolded, lying there in a sleeping bag."

"That's great. If they don't want her to see anything, that means they plan to let her go."

Lori dug her fingers into his arm. "Curt, we can get her out of there."

July 17—12:15 A.M.

Lori knelt beside the metal ring and attacked the knot in the rope. "Leave it," Curt said. "Let's go."

"There's no time to go get help. Right now Pauline's in there by herself. We'd better get her out while we can."

"I thought you meant—"

"We just don't have time. Besides, it's better this way." She moved back from the ring. "Give me a hand here. My fingers are a little stiff."

Curt shifted his hat so that the light shone on the knot. "Are you sure about this?"

"It'll work," Lori said. "No problem. We'll just lower the rope into the Cathedral Room. I'll climb down and wake up Pauline, and we'll be back up the rope in half a minute."

"What do I do?" He yanked the rope free of the ring.

"Nothing—if we're lucky. If Pauline has been drugged or anything, you'll have to help me haul her up out of there." She took the rope from him and began feeding one end through the ring. "We'll climb down the double rope, then pull it down."

Curt took off his hat and shone his light over the edge. "If we take down the rope, how do we get back up here?"

"It's not that big a drop," Lori said. "I can stand on your shoulders and reach the ring."

"Maybe."

"Don't worry. We'll try it before we pull down the rope." She settled her hat on her head. "You want to go first, or shall I?"

"I thought ladies always went first."

"Maybe in Brazil."

"Bolivia," he said, reaching down for the ropes.

"Be sure you keep hold of both ropes," she said.

"Yeah, yeah." He put one leg over the edge, then couldn't hold himself back. He grabbed the two strands tightly as he slid off the ledge. His arms seemed to be yanked out of their sockets, and the rope zipped through his hands.

His feet smacked down, jolting his whole body. He staggered backward but caught himself before he fell.

Lori's light swept over him. "You all right?" she whispered.

Curt blew on his burning hands. "I'm terrific."

She came down the rope, hand over hand. "Did you hurt yourself?"

"Nah."

"You sure didn't waste any time going down." She turned toward the rope. "Come here and give me a hand. I want to be sure I can reach the ring."

The rope hung about a foot away from a sheer rock face. "Nothing to hold on to," Curt said.

"Stand by the rope," she said. "I can kind of use the rock for balance. Now give me a boost."

Curt leaned forward and locked his fingers together. Lori put one foot in his cupped hands, then said, "Here we go." She raised herself, placed her other foot on his shoulder, then straightened up. He grabbed her knees to steady her. She shifted her feet, then whispered, "Coming down." She bent her knees until she was squatting on his shoulders. "I can't quite reach. This time put up your hands and give me a foothold."

She was straightening up again before he could answer. He could feel her legs shaking. Once she was steady, he raised his hands slowly until they were in front of her knees. He shoved the heels of his hands together and waited.

He felt her weight shift to his left shoulder. He bent his knees slightly, to keep his balance. Then her foot was in his hands, and she was moving upward. He clenched his teeth and held his arms rigid. He could feel her twisting around. Then she whispered, "Okay," and her foot slid out of his hands.

Curt smiled as he stepped back and watched Lori climb down the ropes. Suddenly it all seemed possible. He pictured the three of them strolling into the store and giving the reporters a real story.

He helped Lori coil the rope into a figure eight. When they were finished, she reached for the loop, but he threw it over his shoulder. "You don't have to do everything," he said.

She led the way through the mounds of rock that covered the floor of the room. Curt had trouble getting his bearings. The rocks blocked his view, and his light threw shadows everywhere.

Lori stopped between two mounds and came close to whisper in his ear. "Turn off your light here."

They picked their way through the loose rocks. Lori held her hat in her hand and shone her light on their feet. The glow in front of them grew brighter.

Lori squatted down and duck-walked into a low passageway. By the time they had to switch to their hands and knees, they didn't need her light.

She motioned Curt forward. "There's about ten more feet," she whispered. "Take a look."

Curt crawled past her. The ceiling of the Cathedral Room was straight in front of him. He crept onto a ledge and peered around. He was on the north wall, about ten feet from the top. Glancing right and left, he figured he was just above the Popeye formation.

In the center of the ledge was another iron ring. Putting his hand through it, Curt crept to the edge and looked down. His stomach tightened as he spotted Pauline far below, her dark hair spread out above the sleeping bag. She looked small and helpless and alone.

He crept away from the ledge. Lori was sitting on the ground in the passage, tying knots in the rope. "This'll make it easier to climb," she whispered. "Go back and keep an eye out."

He watched the floor of the cave until Lori crawled up beside him. She tied one end of the rope to the ring, then slid the other end over the edge. When the rope was gone, she took off her hat and set it at the far corner of the ledge, then unclipped her battery pack and placed it in the hat. She gave Curt a thumbs-up sign and reached for the rope.

Remembering his own trouble, Curt held her back foot until the other one was free. Then he eased it over the side.

He couldn't lean out far enough to watch her climb down, so he sat back and waited, listening to the swishing sound of her clothes brushing against the rope. He hoped that sound wasn't as loud as it seemed.

When the rope quit shaking, he reached out and lifted it. Lori was down. He leaned forward so that he could see Pauline. She hadn't moved. Then the rope began to quiver again.

A minute later he helped Lori back onto the ledge. "Pull up the rope," she whispered, reaching for her hat.

Once the rope was coiled on the ledge, Lori crawled back into the passage, motioning for him to follow. When they reached the spot where they could stand up, she pointed straight ahead. Curt flipped on his light and followed her over piles of rubble. She stopped at a reasonably flat spot, knelt down, and moved a few rocks aside. "This is about the best we can do," she whispered, sitting down and turning off her light.

"Looks good to me." Curt settled himself beside her before flipping off his light. Even so, the darkness swept over him like cold water. "What happened down there?"

"Those guys are right out in the passage. I guess they can see the cave door and the inside of the Cathedral Room at the same time. They were in their sleeping bags, but one of them was still moving around. I figured we'd be smart to wait an hour or so."

"Yeah." Curt held the luminous dial of his watch close to his face. It was twenty to one. "You think we ought to go get help?"

"It'd take too long. We'll wait an hour, then go ahead."

"Besides, you'd rather do it yourself, right?"

"I just want to get Pauline out of there." She nudged him. "You want half a candy bar?"

"I'd rather have half a pizza, but I'll take it." Reaching out for the candy, his hand brushed her hair. He was suddenly aware of how close she was. "Where is it?"

Lori took his hand and placed the candy in it. "I'll buy you a pizza later."

When he finished the candy, he stretched out, one leg bumping her. "Sorry," he mumbled.

"Don't get too comfortable," she said. "We don't want to go to sleep."

"There's no use for both of us to stay awake," he said. "So you just wake me up when you're ready to go."

She poked him in the ribs. "No way. I'm serious. I could fall asleep in no time. And I'd probably wake up about noon tomorrow."

"Sounds good to me," he muttered.

She poked him again. "Cut it out. Come on. We've got to stay awake. Let's talk."

"You talk. I'll listen."

"I don't trust you," she said. "You talk."

"What about?"

"I don't know. Anything. Tell me about your family."

"Not much to tell. There's just my dad and me. My mother died a long time ago."

"You want to talk about her?"

"No."

"What's your dad like?"

"He's like you. He takes things too seriously." Lori gave him a light poke in the ribs. "He's always getting involved in some project. Works about sixteen hours a day, and he's never satisfied."

"Wanda says he's doing important work."

"I guess."

"You don't think it's important?"

"Oh, it's great—for everybody else. But what does he get out of it? He's a nervous wreck—always rushing around, always yelling. He never has any fun, and he's not even making any money."

"But at least he's doing something that matters." She sounded angry.

Curt leaned back and sighed. "I guess."

"What about you?" she asked after a minute. "What do you want to do?"

He yawned. "I don't know."

"Come on. Don't flake out on me. What would you *really* like to do? Don't you have some dreams?"

"Yeah. Right now I'm dreaming about eating a pizza."

She gave him a push. "Cut that out."

"It's your turn to talk. Tell me about *your* dreams."

"No big secret. I want to play basketball for a good college. And then what I'd really like to do is play on the Olympic team."

"That's not a bad start," he said.

"After that, I want to go to medical school."

"I've got the picture. I can see you living in a big house on a hill and driving to the office in your Cadillac, with your Olympic gold medal around your neck."

"Forget the big house and car," she said. "I don't need that stuff."

"You'll get used to it."

"Look, I want to go into medicine so I can make a difference. Is there anything wrong with that? I don't want to be one of these people who gets to be forty years old and starts wondering what his life is all about and then just—" She stopped for a minute, then asked, "You know what my father is doing right now?"

"Wanda said he lives in New Mexico."

"He's living in a shack and polishing rocks to sell to tourists."

"Maybe he's happy," Curt said.

"That's the thing of it. He isn't. He's bored again. I can tell by his letters. He's thinking about going to Florida. He knows somebody with a boat down there."

"That doesn't sound so bad."

"He's just killing time. That's what he's done his whole life." She sighed. "He was an accountant. He didn't really want to be one. But he was pretty good with numbers, and it was a way to make a lot of money. So we had the big house and the cars and all the goodies. But it wasn't enough. He was always doing something else. For a while it was skiing and then he ran marathons. Then three years ago he threw some clothes in the car and drove off."

"That's rough," Curt muttered.

"People felt sorry for Mom, but she did okay. Right away she got the job as manager here, and she's working part-time for a degree in geology. My dad's the pitiful one. He just drifts around, killing time."

"Maybe it's not as bad as that," Curt said.

Lori snorted. "Maybe it's worse. Anyway, I don't want to live like that. I want my life to mean something. If I can't get into medical school, I'll find something else. And it won't be polishing rocks." She shifted her legs, bumping against Curt. "It's cold when you're not moving around."

"I'm glad you brought me this sweatshirt," he said.

Lori moved up close to him, burying her head against his shoulder. "Don't go getting ideas. I'm just cold."

"I don't believe a word of it. You're just after my body."

She jabbed him in the ribs. "It's your turn to talk. I'm exhausted."

Curt awoke with a jerk, smacking his head against a rock. Lori's arm was wrapped around his waist, and her head lay against his chest. He eased his arm free and lifted his watch up to his eyes. It was three forty-five.

"Lori." He shook her shoulder.

Lori stiffened and pulled away. "What's the matter?"

"We went to sleep. It's almost four o'clock."

"Oh no." She pushed away from him and stood up. She grabbed her hat and turned on her light. "Let's go."

Curt jumped up and followed her over the piles of rubble back to the main passage. One of his legs was asleep.

When they reached the ledge overlooking the Cathedral Room, Lori took a quick look around, then fed the rope over the edge. She handed Curt her hat and battery pack. "Here goes," she whispered. She reached over the side, got a grip on the rope, and eased herself off the ledge. Curt held her left foot until her right leg was clear.

Curt stretched out on his stomach and peered over the edge. Pauline didn't seem to have moved. Below him he could hear the swishing of Lori's clothes against the rope. She was making too much noise.

Three minutes. That was all they needed. In three minutes they would have Pauline up there on the ledge, and the whole nightmare would be over. He couldn't wait to see the look on Sheriff Quinlan's face when the three of them came marching into the store.

Lori crept across the floor. She knelt down beside Pauline and put her hand over Pauline's mouth. Pauline jerked away and sat up. "No!" she screamed.

Lori dashed back toward the rope. Pauline, the blindfold still in place, turned her head from side to side. Once the rope began to shake, Curt slid back into the passageway to give Lori plenty of room.

"Stop! Stop!" It was a male voice, but high-pitched. A broad-shouldered man wearing jeans and a white sweatshirt came running into the Cathedral Room, his arms straight out in front of him. Clutched in his hands was a short-barreled pistol.

"What's going on?" Pauline cried out. "What is it?"

"Hold it!" the man yelled. He stopped and raised the pistol toward the ledge.

"I didn't do anything," Pauline shouted.

The man squared his shoulders and steadied his aim. "Hold it!" he yelled. Curt clenched his teeth, waiting for the shot.

Lori's hand reached up and grasped the iron ring. Curt grabbed her wrist and pulled her forward. She scrambled up onto the ledge. "Keep back," she whispered.

"Get over here." It was a second male voice, deeper than the first. A man in a black sweatshirt was crouched in the entrance to the Cathedral Room.

"What's going on?" Pauline called out. "Please tell me what's going on."

The two men (Curt thought of them as Black and White) huddled together in the entryway. They were surprisingly young, probably in their early twenties. Black, who was doing most of the talking, grabbed the pistol from White and stepped back out of sight. "We're going to move Pauline Thomas," he shouted. "Don't try to stop us, or she'll get hurt."

"Please," Pauline called. "Who is it?"

"It's okay, Pauline," Lori shouted.

Pauline turned in their direction. "Lori?"

"Don't worry," Lori called. "Your dad's taking care of things, and you'll be out of here pretty soon."

White walked across the room, glancing toward the ledge every few steps. He bent over and hoisted Pauline to her feet. She was handcuffed, with the cuffs behind her back. "Hang in there," Lori yelled as Pauline was led away. White disappeared from view, then came back and carried away the sleeping bag and the air mattress.

"Pull up the rope," Curt whispered to Lori.

Lori shook her head. "It won't help. You stay back out of sight. No matter what happens, don't let them know you're up here."

Black stepped into the Cathedral Room and looked up toward them. The pistol was dangling from his hand. "Get down here," he said. "Right now."

Lori didn't move.

"I mean it," Black yelled.

Lori stayed where she was.

Black moved back toward the entranceway. "I've had enough of this," he said. "If you're not down here in ten seconds, we're going to cut off one of Pauline Thomas's ears."

July 17—4:00 A.M.

"No!" Lori shouted.

Black smiled and raised his pistol toward the ledge. He was thin, with dark hair and narrow eyes that seemed to be boring right into Curt. "Get down here," he yelled. "If you don't—"

"I'm coming down," Lori called. "Don't hurt her."

Black moved backward. "Throw down your gun."

"I don't have one," Lori said. She looked back at Curt, then reached for the rope and slid off the ledge.

"The rest of you come out where I can see you," Black shouted. "Right now."

"There's nobody else up there," Lori answered, sounding out of breath.

"I don't have time for games."

"I came in by myself," Lori said, her voice cracking "I couldn't get anybody to come with me."

"Put your hands against the wall," Black shouted, backing toward the entrance. "Go ahead and search her." White stepped into the room, glanced up at the ledge, then ran across the floor.

"I don't have anything," Lori said.

"Nothing," White called after a minute.

"Get back here," Black said. White ducked his head

and ran out. Then Black stepped back into the room. "You'd better tell your friends to come down."

"There's nobody up there," Lori said. "I told the sheriff about the new entrance and showed it to two deputies, but they didn't take me seriously. They wanted to—"

"Where is it?" Black snapped.

"What?"

"The new entrance. Where is it?"

"Down the hill from the one that's sealed. On the north side, in the middle of the elderberries. My mom and I found it and then cleared it out."

"Where's it come in?"

"The big room up above—just like the original."

Black shook his head. "You wouldn't come in here all by yourself."

"I tried to get the stupid deputies to come, but they wouldn't. And they wouldn't let me go either. I had to wait till everybody was asleep, then sneak back up there."

Black looked toward the ledge and yelled, "Hey, come down right now, or we'll shoot this girl."

"Please," Lori said. "I told you. There's nobody up there."

"You've got five seconds," Black shouted.

Curt lay in the same spot, wishing he could crawl forward far enough to look down. He wanted to see Lori's face.

"One, two, three," Black called out, then paused. "Four." He held the pistol straight out in front of him.

Curt slid forward. The guy sounded crazy enough to shoot her.

"There's nobody there," Lori yelled. "Please. There's nobody there."

Curt stopped where he was. He was sure Lori had meant that for him.

"Five," Black yelled.

Curt bit down hard.

"There's nobody there," Lori said again, quieter this time.

"You're an idiot," Black said, lowering his arm. "You came in here all by yourself without even bringing a gun? What were you trying to prove?"

"I just wanted to make sure Pauline was all right."

"She was doing fine until you came along and scared her." He waved with the pistol. "Let's go."

After they were gone, Curt slid forward a few inches and stared down at the Cathedral Room floor. He'd have to wait until those two were asleep. Black had that pistol, and there were hand grenades somewhere. The tour group had seen them.

Five minutes later Black came back into the Cathedral Room. He was wearing a silver hardhat. "You stay out of the way," he said over his shoulder. He crossed the room, moving out of sight below Curt. Then Curt heard him grunt, and the rope rubbed back and forth on the rock.

Curt slid backward into the passageway. Black was coming.

Curt didn't have room to turn around in the narrow passage. He raised up on his hands and knees and crawled backward, keeping his eyes on the lighted opening. His boots scraped over rocks, and once his hardhat banged against the ceiling. He couldn't worry about noise, though. He had to get out of there.

When he figured that he had gone far enough, he threw a hand up behind him and smacked his knuckles on rock. He crawled several more feet and tried again.

When his hand didn't hit anything, he twisted around and scrambled to his feet, keeping his head low.

After looking into the Cathedral Room lights, he couldn't see a thing. He flipped on his light to get his bearings. Just ahead of him was a mound of rocks. If he crouched behind it, he might be able to surprise somebody coming through the low passage. It wasn't much of a plan, but it was better than crawling into a hole and waiting for Black to find him. He scrambled past the mound and turned off his light.

He was still catching his breath when a shaft of light bounced off the rocks in front of him. He took a deep breath and held it. Black was entering the passageway.

The light moved back and forth slowly. Curt shifted his weight from one foot to the other and tried not to think about his cramping muscles. Then the light was gone. Curt shook his head and stared into the darkness. Was Black gone, or was he lying there in the passage, waiting for Curt to move? Curt leaned forward and listened. All he could hear was his own breathing.

Soon the rocks around him began to take shape as his eyes got used to the dim light. He decided not to move for fifteen minutes. He settled himself on the ground and waited, checking his watch again and again. After ten minutes of silence, he slid forward until he could peer into the opening. Nobody was there. He took a deep breath and crawled toward the ledge.

Just as he reached the ledge, he realized that Black could be waiting out there. But by then it was too late to change his mind. He clenched his teeth and slid forward.

The ledge was empty. Even Lori's hat, which had been sitting on the far side, was gone.

Curt crept forward and peered down into the Cathe-

dral Room. A green camp stove sat in the middle of the
floor, surrounded by cartons and cans. White was sitting
next to the stove, using his fingers to eat pears from a
can. Curt thought White's hands were an odd pale
color, then realized he was wearing gloves.

Curt's stomach rumbled. Right then he would have
paid a hundred dollars for a can of pears.

White tipped up the can and drank the juice, then
hurled the can against the far wall.

"That's really cute," Black said. He was stretched out
on a sleeping bag at the entrance to the room. Curt
figured that Black could see the cave door from there.

"Drop dead." White opened another can of pears.

"Open one for me," Black said.

White slid a pear half into his mouth. "Get your
own."

Black came across the room and opened a can. He
squatted down and ate from the can with a plastic fork.
Curt saw that he was wearing gloves too. "Quit acting
like a two-year-old. We're doing all right."

"Yeah, everything's wonderful," White shouted. "You
and your hotshot plans."

Black lit the stove. "I think I'll heat up some tea."

White threw his can aside and drank from a bottle of
Perrier. "I don't care what you say. We're dead in the
water. Nobody was going to know what we looked like,
right? Wear disguises and keep the rich brat blindfolded. And then this cow comes sliding down the rope
like Sheena of the Jungle." He raised the bottle into the
air.

"You break that bottle, and you're going to pick up
every single piece," Black shouted.

White glared at him, then set down the bottle.
"We're dead."

Black picked up a pot and put it on the stove. "Quit whining, Artie. You get on my nerves."

"We're gonna get caught," Artie said, his voice rising. "I just know we are."

"Will you stop it?" Black shouted. "Nothing's changed. We're doing fine." He popped open two cans of tea and poured them into the pot. "Look, as long as our schedule's messed up, we might as well feed Pauline too. Open some fruit, will you?"

Artie mumbled something, then picked up the can opener. "That girl knows what we look like."

"Shut up, Artie," Black said quietly. "You do what I tell you, and we'll be okay. And right now I'm telling you to open those cans."

Artie grumbled, but he opened the cans and carried them out of the room. Black poured tea into a cup and carried it back to his sleeping bag. He set down his cup and took the pistol out of his belt. He pulled back the hammer and aimed at the wall in front of him. Then he lowered the hammer and set the pistol beside him.

Artie came back and opened another can. "I might as well give the other one something to eat too," he said, grabbing two bottles of Perrier.

"Good," Black said. "Just don't touch those knots."

Black drank two cups of tea before Artie came back and crawled into his sleeping bag. "Might as well get some rest, I guess."

Black stood up and left the room, the pistol dangling from his right hand. A few minutes later he stamped back into the room and dropped to his knees beside Artie's sleeping bag. He shoved the pistol against the base of Artie's skull. "I'd be doing the human race a favor if I pulled the trigger."

"Don't," Artie yelled. "Come on, Frank. Cut it out."

"You're hopeless," Frank said. He stood up and shoved the pistol into his belt.

Artie rolled over. "What's the matter?"

"You idiot. Another five minutes and that girl would have been loose."

Artie looked away. "I'm sorry, Frank."

Frank shook his head. "I'm trying to get us out of this mess, and you do something dumb like that. What'd she do—cry and say her hands hurt?"

"I'm sorry."

"How could you be so stupid? You watched me tie her up. You saw all the trouble I went to, getting everything tight but not hurting her. And then you go in there and do something like that."

"I said I was sorry." Artie sounded peeved. "What else do you want?"

"Just do exactly what I tell you, all right? And not one thing else. Do you think you can handle that?" Frank walked over to his own sleeping bag and flopped down. He set the pistol beside his head.

"Frank," Artie said after a minute, "you didn't hurt her, did you?"

"She's fine. Now shut up and get some sleep."

Curt turned and crawled headfirst into the passage. If he could get past that one spot, he could make it out of the cave and bring the sheriff's men back with him.

He duck-walked past the mound where he had hidden, wondering if his plan would have worked. Probably not, he decided. Frank would have been moving too slowly and flashing his light everywhere.

When he reached the place where he could stand up, Curt studied his position. He hadn't worried much about direction before. He had just followed Lori. He started through the piles of rubble, searching for something that looked familiar.

When he couldn't go any farther, he looked back at the glow behind him and decided that he had gone too far to the left. He headed back toward the glow, then picked his way between two mounds. A minute later he was looking at the rock wall and the ledge above.

Curt stood at the base of the wall and stared upwards. The ledge wasn't that far above him. Lori had been able to reach it by standing on his shoulders. He moved his light up and down the rock face, looking for cracks or ridges—anything that would give him a hold. If he could get six feet off the ground, he'd be able to reach the ledge.

He stood on his tiptoes and dug his fingers into a small crack. Then he used his boot to locate a foothold. Finding one, he hoisted himself up. Once he was balanced, he raised one hand and swept the smooth rock. His other hand slipped, and he slid back to the ground.

He held his hat high above his head and swept the light across the face of the rock. Seeing nothing helpful, he stepped to his left and moved the light up and down in a careful pattern.

Nothing. It was impossible—a sheer rock face with nothing to hold on to. He only needed to climb six feet, but it might as well have been six miles.

He felt his chest tighten. The air around him seemed stale. He looked toward the Cathedral Room and then back at the rock face. He and Lori should have gone for help right away. Lori should never have gone down the rope. He should have— But now there was nothing he could do. He was trapped.

July 17—12:50 P.M.

Curt awoke with a jerk, his heart pounding. He moved his wrist in front of his eyes and cupped his hand around the watch dial. It was almost one o'clock in the afternoon. He had been asleep nearly seven hours.

He crawled forward and peered down into the Cathedral Room. Then he slumped against the rock. They were still there. Artie was curled up in his sleeping bag, and Frank was lying on his bag, reading a magazine.

Curt scooted backward and rubbed his aching knees. Pure dumb luck. He had stopped to rest for a minute and had conked out for seven hours, but apparently he hadn't missed much. And the sleep had probably helped him, although he still felt so dopey he could hardly keep his head up. He wished he had some water. He didn't care about food anymore, but his tongue was fuzzy and his throat was raw.

The next hours crawled by. Curt dozed a few minutes at a time, watched the two men doing nothing, then dozed again. He kept looking at the case of Perrier. He imagined himself prying off the cap, tilting up the bottle, and letting the water roll over his tongue.

At four thirty Frank got up and heated some tea. He opened a can of fruit and ate it slowly with a fork. Then he opened some more cans and dumped them into an aluminum pot. A rich smell of spiced tomatoes drifted up to Curt. He ground his teeth and tried to think of other things.

Frank dumped some of the food onto a paper plate, then set the pot beside Artie. Artie mumbled something and turned away. Frank sat on the ground and ate from the paper plate. "Get up and eat," he said.

Artie grumbled something.

"Come on. Get moving. We've got things to do."

Artie dragged himself out of the sleeping bag and walked to the bottled water. He opened a bottle and took a drink. Then he poured water into his hand and rubbed it on his face and into his hair.

Curt ground his teeth and tried to swallow. He scooted back from the ledge. There was no point in watching those two eat.

Tonight, he decided. Tonight he'd go down the rope. He couldn't wait any longer. He'd wait until midnight or so, let them go to sleep. Then he'd take his chances and go down.

"Hurry up and finish," Frank said.

"What time is it?"

"Ten after five."

Remembering that five o'clock was the time for the first money to be delivered, Curt crawled forward once more. He saw Artie stand up and throw a can to one side. "Why didn't you say so?" Artie shouted.

Frank put the pistol in his belt. "I just did."

"I didn't know it was five o'clock already. I'd better get ready." Artie knelt beside his sleeping bag and put on a baseball cap and dark glasses.

"We're right on schedule," Frank said. "Let me fix that beard."

After helping Artie put on the beard, Frank raised

Artie's white sweatshirt, wrapped a sleeping bag around his chest, and pulled the sweatshirt down over it.

"Do I look okay?" Artie asked.

"Perfect. Just grab the stuff and get back inside. All they'll see is a fat guy with a beard. Your mother wouldn't recognize you."

"But what about that girl, Frank?"

"Quit worrying. Let's go get rich."

Curt looked down into the empty room. He grabbed the rope, then let it go again. Even if he had time to get down, there was no place to hide. It was better to wait.

He heard them shouting and laughing as they came up the passage. "Clockwork," Frank said, trotting into the room. "The whole thing." He and Artie were each carrying a brown leather suitcase.

Artie yanked away his beard and threw his dark glasses on the ground. "Let's take a look."

Frank set his case on his sleeping bag and opened the lid. "Green—my favorite color. Just look at that stuff."

Artie set his case alongside and undid the snaps. "Wow."

Frank smacked Artie on the shoulder. "Now what do you say? Didn't I tell you it'd work?"

"You sure it's not counterfeit?"

"They wouldn't dare." Frank turned the suitcase upside down. The packets of bills formed a green mound in front of him. "Look at it." He scooped up a handful of packets. "You'd work all year for this much."

Artie picked up a packet and thumbed it. "Are we gonna count it?"

Frank laughed. "We don't have to. We're dealing with old Raymond Thomas himself. He's not going to shortchange us." He pulled something out of the other case. "He even wrote us a letter. It's addressed to the Brotherhood of New Freedom." He tore open the envelope. "Listen to this: 'We will follow your instructions exactly. Please take care of Pauline.' He doesn't say anything about that other stupid girl. They probably don't even know she's in here. And he says if we need anything else, we should leave a note outside the cave door. What do you think? Think we ought to ask for another suitcase full of money?" He laughed and tossed the note aside.

Artie ran his hands over the pile. "I didn't think there'd be so much."

"It's mostly twenties. They take up a lot of space. No problem, though. Go get the vest."

Artie got up and started toward the entrance. "Hey, Frank?"

"Yeah?"

"What are we gonna do?"

"Follow the plan. What do you think?"

"What about the girl?"

"Will you shut up about her? Go get that vest."

Artie stood in the entrance. "You're not gonna hurt her, are you?"

"Get the vest, Artie."

"You said nobody'd get hurt. I wouldn't have come otherwise." Artie turned and left the room. Frank raised his pistol and pointed it at Artie's back. He muttered something, then stuffed the pistol back into his belt.

The vest looked like white canvas, with black pockets sewn all over it. The two men spent several minutes stuffing the pockets with the packets of bills. When they were finished, Frank stripped off his black sweatshirt and put on the bulky vest. Then he picked up a coil of rope and wrapped that around the outside of the vest. When he pulled on his sweatshirt again, he looked like a football player in full pads.

"If you want anything else to eat or drink, get it now," Frank said. "I'll go take care of the door."

"What about the girl? What are you going to do with her?"

Frank spun around. "What do *you* want to do with her, Artie? I'm curious. Let's hear your ideas on the subject."

Artie shook his head. "I don't have any ideas, Frank."

Frank sighed. "That's what I thought." He turned and left the room.

Artie opened a can of pears and ate them with his fingers, then drank another bottle of Perrier. He dug through some equipment and brought out a yellow hardhat. He clipped a battery pack to his belt, checked the light, and adjusted the hat. Curt shifted around on the ledge, ready to crawl back into the hole if Artie should start up the rope.

When Frank came back, he had Lori with him. Her face was flushed, and a strand of hair hung down over one cheek. She walked awkwardly, her body bent forward. It took a minute for Curt to realize that her hands were tied behind her.

"How you doing?" Artie asked her.

"I'm okay," she said.

"You want something to drink?"

"Yes, please."

"Here you go," Frank said. He took a knife from his pocket and tossed it to Artie. "Cut her loose."

When her hands were free, Lori rubbed her wrists. "Thank you," she told Artie.

"Help yourself to the water," Frank said. "Artie, take

your stuff and go out by the door." Artie seemed about to speak but left without saying anything. Lori opened a bottle of Perrier and drank it down.

"Have a seat," Frank said, sitting down on the ground. He kept his hand on the pistol in his belt.

Lori sat on Artie's sleeping bag. "Would it be all right if I ate something?"

Frank shrugged. "Go ahead."

Lori reached for a can of fruit. "Thank you."

Frank shook his head while she opened the can. "I can't believe it," he said finally. "Perfect plan, and you come along and mess it up."

Lori drank the juice from the can, then picked up a plastic spoon. "What can I say?"

"Everything went like clockwork. We got the money, and we're ready to go. By the time anybody out there realizes there's something wrong, we'll be five hundred miles from here."

Lori looked at him. "What about the chauffeur and the jet and all that?"

Frank smiled. "Window dressing. We're leaving right away, and those people are going to be sitting out there watching an empty hole. You see how good it is? Nobody knows what we look like, and nobody will know how we did it. Pauline Thomas will be America's sweetheart. Probably get her picture on *Time* magazine. Her father'll be so happy he won't even miss the money, and he's probably insured anyway. So everybody comes out ahead." He shook his head. "It was perfect. And then you had to come along and foul up everything."

Lori took a bite of peaches and shrugged. "You want me to say I'm sorry?"

"That's the way my luck goes," Frank said. "How was I supposed to know somebody had discovered a new

entrance? And how was I supposed to know you'd be
stupid enough to come in all by yourself? It would have
been one thing if you'd brought in ten guys with machine guns or something." He stopped and shook his
head again. "It just kills me to think that one stupid girl
messed up everything."

"You got the money, didn't you?"

"It's different now," Frank said. "It was all going to be
a joke, see? You know that D. B. Cooper—the guy who
hijacked a plane, then parachuted out with the ransom
money? It was going to be like that. Nobody was going
to get hurt. We've been really nice to Pauline Thomas. I
even brought in wristbands so the handcuffs wouldn't
hurt her. The only bad time she's had was when you
came along and scared her."

Lori opened a bottle of Perrier and drank from it.

"But that would have been too easy. You had to come
along." He pulled the pistol out of his belt. "I probably
ought to kill you. Why not? You're nothing to me."

Curt reached for a rock. He doubted that he could hit
Frank; the angle was too strange. But he had to do
something.

"You wouldn't want—" Lori began.

Frank held up his free hand. "Right. I don't want to.
It would mess up everything. Then it wouldn't be a joke
anymore. But I don't need a witness either."

Curt held the rock in his hand and waited.

"I could just give them lousy descriptions," Lori said.
"You know. About average height, average weight.
Like that."

"That's what you say now. You might change your
mind later on."

"I wouldn't. I promise."

"But we could never be sure." Frank shook his head

and used his free hand to open a bottle of Perrier. "It's a mess." He took a long drink. "It's not just you, see? My partner'd go to pieces if you got killed, so I'd have to kill him too."

Lori leaned toward him. "Trust me. I won't cause any problems."

Frank smiled at her. "You've got three lives in your hands—yours, my partner's, and Pauline Thomas's. Tomorrow I'll make a phone call and say that I'm sending directions how to get the cave door open without blowing the place apart. You give me any trouble, and we'll forget about sending that letter."

"I won't cause any trouble," Lori said.

"Of course, a bomb squad might be able to get in without the place going up. I don't think so, though. And if it blows, the whole mountain's likely to come down."

Lori held up her hands. "I'll do anything you say."

"I know." Frank stood up and put on his silver hardhat. "I brought your hat down for you. You'll need it. We've got some heavy duty caving ahead of us."

From outside, Artie called, "Is everything okay, Frank?"

"Yeah," Frank said. "She wants to come with us."

After Lori had her hat on, she reached for her bottle of Perrier. She tilted it up, her eyes moving toward the ledge. Then she looked toward Frank. "How do we get out?"

"Just follow me." He walked out of the room, and Lori followed. Artie ran in, grabbed another bottle of Perrier, pried off the cap, and ran out with it.

Curt dropped the rock he had been holding and grabbed the rope. Remembering the trouble he had had before, he put his hands just above a knot so that they wouldn't slide. When he rolled off the ledge, his body jerked downward, but he was ready this time. He held tightly to the rope and wrapped his legs around it, searching for a knot with his feet.

He worked his way down the rope from one knot to the next. When he was a few feet from the floor, he let go and dropped. He bent his knees as he landed, but he still fell forward.

Scrambling up, he dashed across the room and grabbed the bottle opener. He pried the caps off three bottles of Perrier and drank them down. He glanced at the food but decided not to take the time.

He ran out of the Cathedral Room and looked toward the entrance. Then he looked to his left and right, down the empty passages. He didn't know which direction to take.

10

July 17—6:30 P.M.

Curt took the passage to his right. Pauline had to be around there somewhere. He trotted past the Popcorn Room. Bottles and cans had been tossed next to one wall.

He dashed through the Grecian Room and along the twisting path toward the Frozen Falls. "Who is it?" Pauline called out.

"Me," Curt said, stepping into the Falls Corridor.

Pauline, wrapped in a sleeping bag, was sitting with her back to the wall, just to the left of the Frozen Falls formation. "Curt," she burst out. "Oh, Curt, it's so good to see you." She reached toward him with one arm.

Curt dropped to his knees beside the sleeping bag and gave her a hug. She wrapped the arm around his neck. Her other arm was handcuffed to the electrical conduit for the cave lights. "Are you all right?" he asked.

"I am now. I was so scared." She gave him another hard squeeze, then let go of him.

He slid back and sat on the ground. "I wish I could get you loose."

"Don't worry about it," she said. "Now that my hands are in front of me and that blindfold's off, I'm fine." She looked at him. "Is Lori with you?"

"No. We came in last night by that upper passage. Those guys caught her when she came down a rope into the Cathedral Room. She thought she could get you out of there."

Pauline sighed. "And I fouled it up by screaming."

"They got Lori, but they didn't know I was up there. But I couldn't do anything until they left. Then I came down the rope."

"Where's Lori?"

"They took her along."

"Where'd they go?"

"I don't know. They must have some other way out."

"Go get some help," Pauline said. "Don't worry about me. I'm doing fine."

"I can't," he said. "The door's wired with explosives."

"What about the way you came in?"

"Can't do it." He scrambled to his feet. "Look, I hate to leave you here, but I've got to go after them."

"Go ahead," Pauline said. "I've got food and water and magazines to read. I'll be fine."

"Do you have any idea how somebody might get out?"

"They didn't come this way. That's all I know. The one who talks brought the food and stuff, changed the handcuffs, and told me not to take off the blindfold for five minutes. That's the last I heard from them."

"I'll be back as soon as I can," Curt said, starting away.

"Good luck," Pauline called.

Curt ran past the Cathedral Room, then lowered his head and dashed down the narrow passage toward the Pink Room. He only thought about noise when he was almost to the end of the passage. He had been clumping along like an elephant, so worried about catching up that he hadn't really thought about their hearing him. He stopped and listened. He couldn't hear anything except his own heart. But they could be sitting up ahead in the Pink Room, holding a gun on Lori and waiting for the elephant to show his face.

He tiptoed along the rest of the passage, then eased his head around the corner. He let out the breath he had been holding and stepped into the open. The Pink Room was empty.

Curt sat down on the floor, disgusted with himself. If only he had taken a chance and come down the rope earlier.

What was he going to do now? Sit in the Falls Corridor with Pauline and read magazines until somebody rescued them? Or maybe he could try to open the cave door and blow up the mountain.

He studied the low ceiling of the Pink Room. The place was just as boring as ever—a box of a room without a single spectacular formation. The guides tried to get the tour groups excited about the rosy color, and then they shut off the lights for an experience of total darkness. But it was hard to hide the fact that this section of the cave was just a time killer.

Glancing around, Curt realized he had never looked at the room closely. He had just come in with tour groups and gone out again. On the far wall was a dark spot he hadn't noticed before. He jumped up and ran over there. It was only a shadow.

Curt kept looking around him. Something was different. Something was out of place. But he couldn't decide what.

He moved back to the entrance and walked in, the way he did five or six times each day. Coming in that way, he immediately spotted the rocks. They hadn't been there before. Two wedge-shaped rocks the size of typewriters were propped against a side wall.

He dashed across the room and used both hands to pick up one of the rocks. Nothing. He pushed the other rock aside, knowing it was a waste of effort.

But the rocks hadn't been there before.

He walked back toward the entrance, his eyes sweeping the room. Bits of orange paper lay on the floor in front of him. He knelt down and scooped them up—five tiny squares torn off a piece of heavy orange paper.

A free-drink coupon. That's what those squares had been torn from. Lori had been here.

Curt stood up and looked around. Directly overhead was a section where an egg-shaped portion of the ceiling had fallen away, leaving a dimple three feet across and two feet deep. The tour guides never mentioned that dimple. They didn't want people to start thinking about ceilings falling in.

Curt reached up and ran his hands along the sides of the indentation. He could see rock at the top and rock all the way around. He flipped on his light and held the hardhat as high as he could. On one side, just out of reach, was a narrow shelf, but he could see solid rock just behind it.

But Lori had dropped those bits of coupon. Something must be there.

After tightening the chin strap on his hat, he jumped up, as if he were going to dunk a ball, and grabbed the shelf with both hands. He hung there for a second, then dug in his fingers and chinned himself. He rested his chin on his hands, wishing he had turned on his light.

He worked his elbows up onto the shelf, then wriggled forward. In a minute his weight was resting on his chest, and he was looking straight into a rock wall.

His legs still dangling in the air, he inched forward on his forearms to ease the pressure on his ribs. He banged his right forearm down and thrust the left one forward. Instead of hitting rock, it sank into a hole. His ribs smacked down on the shelf.

Fighting to keep from sliding off the shelf, he shifted his weight back to his right forearm. Then he thrust his left hand out in front of him. Beneath the rock wall that his hardhat was scraping was an opening that dipped down. This was where those wedge-shaped rocks had come from.

Curt reached back with his left hand and turned on his light. Then he ducked his head and wriggled forward into the opening. As he inched along, he pictured himself stuck there, his legs flopping in the air.

Just when he had pulled himself forward far enough to get his knees onto the shelf, the passage turned upward. Soon his body was being bent backward as he worked his way up the incline. He managed to twist his body sideways to relieve the pressure on his spine. Then he reached ahead, dug in his fingers, and hauled himself a few inches upward. *And people pay money to do this,* he thought.

After a few feet the passageway leveled off and expanded enough for him to crawl. Then the ceiling above him disappeared, and he scrambled to his feet. Tied to a rock was a piece of knotted rope that the others must have used to climb out of the Pink Room.

Curt turned away from the rope and glanced around him. His light reflected off the far wall, perhaps twenty feet ahead of him. He picked his way through the rocks that covered the floor, stopping once to study the way he had come. He didn't want to get lost in there.

On the opposite side, the room narrowed into a passageway. Curt headed that way until he saw a second opening off to his right. He veered toward it, wondering how he was supposed to make a decision. He crouched at the opening and let his light play up and down. The passage continued for as far as he could see.

Figuring that he ought to check the other possibility, Curt turned in that direction. As he did so, his light flashed past something on the wall. He jerked his head back. On the left wall was a crooked line of green chalk.

In spite of everything, Curt smiled. He could imagine Lori with her chalk hidden in her fingers, innocently running her hand along the wall. She was amazing.

He ducked his head and trotted down the passage.

As time passed Curt tried to keep his mind on the ground in front of him. "Cool and easy," he kept muttering in that railroad engine chant. He had long since lost any sense of direction. Even though he had left markers for himself, he still wasn't sure he could find his way back out. And how long were his batteries going to last? "Cool and easy. Cool and easy."

He was moving too slowly. He kept having to search around for chalk marks or scrapings on the rocks. The route he was following didn't make any sense at all. When there was a choice between an opening big enough for a truck and a crack eight inches wide, he usually found chalk marks on the crack. And some of those tight passages took forever to get through.

The only encouraging thing was that he had come across a cave-in that the others had had to clear. He could see signs of digging and rocks piled off to the side. That meant that he had gained some time. And he had found a little "L" etched in the fresh dirt, so Lori was still all right.

After crawling along a twisting passageway for what seemed like miles, he emerged into a small room. He stood up and stretched, trying to work the kinks out of his back. As usual, once he quit moving, he was surrounded by absolute silence.

But this time there was a noise—the old familiar sound of boots scraping against rock. Curt jumped back against the wall and turned to his right. A pair of legs was sticking out of a narrow opening.

Curt looked around for a hiding place, then stopped. The legs squirmed forward. Curt realized that the owner of those legs had no idea that Curt was there.

Dropping to his knees beside the wriggling feet, Curt saw that the boots had rawhide laces. He untied the knot in the closer boot and wrapped the lace around his hand.

The legs surged forward. Curt braced himself and held the lace fast. There was another tug, then quick shakes and two more hard tugs. Curt grinned and didn't budge.

The lace went slack as the man wriggled backward. Curt held his hand steady as the lace tightened again, the man tugging in the opposite direction. Curt held the boot in place while the man's other leg slowly emerged from the hole.

When the leg was almost out of the hole, the man began twisting his body around. Curt caught a glimpse of a white sweatshirt. Artie. He wished it had been Frank, but he'd settle for what he could get.

A hand appeared, working its way back toward the boot. Curt didn't move until the hand was almost touching his. Then he grabbed the hand, wrapped the lace around the wrist, and tied it tight. Artie yelled, but his voice was too muffled for Curt to catch the words.

Curt sat down on Artie's other leg and removed the lace from the boot. At first Artie wiggled and tried to kick, but soon he just lay still. Holding the lace in his teeth, Curt pulled Artie out of the hole far enough so that he could catch hold of Artie's other hand. He tied that hand to Artie's belt, then pulled his head out into the open.

Artie lay on the ground and stared up at Curt. "Who are you?"

"Where's your gun?" Curt said.

"I don't have one."

Curt checked his pockets anyway, finding nothing but a small Swiss Army knife. That was a disappointment, but he still had a chance if he acted quickly. "I want you to yell for help," he told Artie. "Yell as loud as you can."

"I already did," Artie said. "Didn't you hear me?"

Curt shoved Artie's head into opening. "Do it. Right now."

"Help!" Artie yelled. "Help!"

Curt pushed him farther into the hole. "Louder."

The sound was muffled, and Curt couldn't tell if Artie was really yelling or not. He shook Artie's shoulders to encourage him.

After a minute Curt pulled Artie out of the way and listened.

"What's the matter?" Frank's voice sounded far off. Looking into the passageway, Curt could see the glow from Frank's light. He figured they were at least thirty feet apart.

"Tell him to come here," Curt whispered. He turned off Artie's light and pulled Artie toward the opening.

"Frank," Artie yelled, "he's got me."

Curt yanked Artie away. "You say one more word,

and I'll cut your throat." He moved back to the hole and shouted, "Hey, Frank."

"Who are you?"

"Quinlan," Curt said, using the first name he thought of. "Sheriff's department."

"How'd you get here?"

"I came down the rope into the Cathedral Room right after you left. Been right behind you all the way." He waited for a minute, but Frank didn't say anything. "Hey, Frank, I've got a deal for you. I'll trade you Artie for that girl."

"I've got a deal for *you*," Frank said. "You let Artie go, or I'll start slicing that girl into little pieces."

Curt didn't answer until he was sure he could control his voice. "Forget it. Keep the girl. I'll get a promotion for bringing Artie back."

"You're bluffing," Frank said. "And I'm not. I'll start with her ear."

"That's your problem. I've done too much stupid crawling to go back empty-handed. I'd rather take the girl back, but Artie's better than nothing."

"What about the money?"

Curt smiled for the first time. "Keep it. It's not my money. I don't want to haul it out of here anyway." He moved away from the hole and turned his light on Artie.

Artie hadn't moved at all. "I've got a cramp in my leg," he whined.

"Good," Curt muttered. He waited a minute, then called, "Frank?"

"Give me a little time."

While he waited, Curt tried to think of a safe way to make the exchange. He still hadn't come up with anything foolproof when Frank yelled, "Hey."

"I'm still here," Curt called.

"It's a deal," Frank said. "But I have to check something out first. There's a passage up ahead that might be blocked. I don't want to get stuck in here. As soon as I make sure we can get through, I'll come back, and we'll trade."

"What are we talking about? How much time?"

"Twenty minutes. Ten minutes up there and ten back. And one more thing: after we trade, you and the girl have to promise to wait an hour before you start back."

"What else are you going to want—my gun and my shoes?"

"Twenty minutes now," Frank said. "And then an hour after we trade."

"All right," Curt said. "I'm ready for a rest anyway."

Once he was sure Frank had gone, Curt turned toward Artie. "Please don't hurt me," Artie said.

"I'm going to tie you up differently," Curt said. "You make one funny move, and you'll be sorry."

"Thanks," Artie said. "My leg hurts bad."

After he was finished with Artie, Curt stuck his head into the opening. He thought he had the exchange figured out. The passageway was narrow for several feet, then widened out. Artie and Lori could squeeze past each other in that middle section while he and Frank stayed out of the way.

Curt backed out of the passage and lay flat on the ground. For the first time since leaving the Cathedral Room, he thought about food.

When twenty-five minutes had passed, Curt moved beside the opening. "Hey, Frank," he called, staring into the empty passageway. "Hey, Frank."

Curt sat back and looked at his watch. What was

taking Frank so long? He had to be coming back. He had to. If he wasn't, why would he have insisted that Curt and Lori wait an hour? Then Curt remembered the instructions for the plane and the limousine and the television cameras—all those details that were just a smoke screen.

Curt snatched up the pocketknife and grabbed Artie's shoulder. "Frank ran out on you," he said.

"No," Artie moaned.

"How much farther do we have to go?"

Artie shook his head. "I don't know."

Curt put the blade of the knife against Artie's throat. "I asked you a question, and I want an answer."

"I don't know. Honest. Please don't hurt me. I don't know. I've never been here before. Frank's the one. He planned it all out."

"What do you think? A half hour? An hour?"

"Don't cut me," Artie whispered. "I don't know. We're supposed to get out by dark. That's all I know. We're supposed to walk back to the cabin in the dark."

"Where's the cabin?"

"It's on Willow Road. I don't know the number or anything. There's a brown mailbox just after you cross the bridge. You go back up a dirt road."

"Roll over," Curt said. He took the batteries out of Artie's battery pack. He might need them before he was through.

Artie rolled onto his back. His eyes shone in the light. "Take me with you. Please."

"I can't."

Artie began to sob. "Don't leave me here in the dark. Please."

"I'm sorry." Curt dropped onto his stomach and started into the hole.

The crazy thing was that he really did feel sorry for that stupid kidnapper.

Once he had squeezed past the tight spot, Curt saw that his plan for the exchange would have worked. The passage was wide enough for two people to pass. But nothing was working the way it should.

And it was his fault. Because of his stupidity, Lori might be dead. Why would Frank keep her after leaving Artie behind?

He scrambled through the passage, his hardhat banging against the ceiling. He came out in a small room where he could almost stand up straight. On every wall were dark holes. He dashed around the room, searching for a sign. After making a full circle, he started again, working more slowly. This time he spotted a tiny smudge of green chalk on the rocks beside one of the openings.

A twisting passageway took him into an open area nearly the size of the Cathedral Room. He worked his way through mounds of rocks to the far side of the room, which gradually narrowed into a corridor. He kept looking for green chalk as he hurried along, but didn't see any. Ahead of him was a mound of white rocks, where there was bound to be another opening. He wasted several minutes crawling over those rocks before he realized that he had reached a dead end.

Back in the main room, he worked his way along the walls. When he spotted a crevice in the wall ahead of him, he ran to it. He stuck his head into it and saw solid rock in front of his nose. He took a step away, then stopped. On the ground beside his shoe were bits of orange paper.

Curt let out a sigh. If he couldn't go in, there was only one direction left—up. He tipped his head back. The crevice ran up the rock for fifteen or twenty feet. Above that was an overhang, blocking his view.

He moved sideways into the crevice and flattened his back against the rock. That left about six inches of space between his face and the rock in front of him. He reached up and found a handhold. He pulled himself up as far as he could, then used his knees to wedge his body in place while he grabbed another handhold.

His arms soon grew rubbery, and his eyes wouldn't focus. He couldn't tell how far he had come, and he didn't dare look down.

He thrust up a hand and smacked his knuckles against rock. He braced himself and rested for a minute before grabbing on to the overhang. Using his knees for leverage, he worked his way up onto a ledge. He collapsed on the rock, but he kept his eyes wide open so that he wouldn't fall asleep.

He sat up and looked around. He was on an outcropping halfway up the wall. He tilted his head back and ran his light up the crevice. He had another fifteen feet to go. Moaning quietly, he brought his head down to check his shoelaces. He jerked his hands away from his body.

The right leg of his jeans was covered with blood. He patted himself, then rolled up his pant leg to check his knee. The skin was red and bruised, but he couldn't find a cut. He stood up quickly, checking his arms and hands.

He turned and moved his light across the ledge. Two feet in front of him was a reddish smear. Beyond that was a dark puddle and more red splotches.

Curt flopped down on the ledge. He was too late. Lori was dead.

Lori! He pictured her standing at the free-throw line with that smug grin on her face.

But where was she? She couldn't have fallen to the floor below. He would have seen her body.

Maybe there was a chance. He worked himself back into the crevice and started upward. Maybe Lori was up there. Maybe.

Handhold by handhold, he worked his way up. "I'm coming, Lori," he whispered. "I'm coming."

He dug his fingers into a crack and pulled himself forward. Feeling his fingers slipping, he raked the rock with his boot. His fingers gave way, and his body slid slowly downward, his face smacking against the rock again and again.

He jerked up his knees, and his backbone banged against the rock. He was tilted backward, but he had stopped sliding. He took a breath and reached up again. "I'm coming, Lori."

When his fingers felt flat rock, he was too weak to pull himself out. He worked his way up the crevice a few inches at a time until he could ease his elbows onto the rock lip. Then he wriggled ahead until his chest was resting on the rock.

Clenching his teeth, he dragged himself forward. His light flashed across a shape on the floor in front of him. "No!" he screamed.

He had found Lori.

11

July 17—9:00 P.M.

Lori's body lay on the floor, ten feet in front of him. Her back was to him, her hands clasped behind her.

"Lori!" Curt scrambled to his feet, banging his hat on the low ceiling. He lowered his head and dashed toward her.

The body started rocking furiously. "Hey," Curt burst out. "You're—" He broke into a laugh that was almost a sob.

When he dropped to his knees beside her, she twisted her head to look up at him. Her cheeks were puffed out, and a wad of white cloth protruded from her mouth. Curt grabbed the wad and pulled it out. Lori sagged back to the floor, taking in huge breaths.

Curt put his hand on her shoulder. "Everything's going to be okay."

"Oh, Curt," she said between gasps, "that thing was suffocating me. I thought I was going to die right here."

He ran his light over her legs. "Are you hurt? I saw blood down there."

"It wasn't mine."

"Let me get you loose." Using Artie's knife, Curt cut the laces on her wrists.

Lori sat up and threw her arms around his neck. Curt lost his balance and toppled to the floor. Lori went with him, her arms still locked around him. They lay in a heap for a while before she pulled back and lifted his hardhat from his head. She turned the hat around and shone the light on Curt's face. "You're beautiful," she said, kissing his cheek.

Curt gently took his hat and placed it back on his head. "Are you okay?" He was surprised to see that her eyes were red and swollen. He had never pictured Lori crying.

"I've been better." She reached out and touched his arm. "I can't believe you're really here."

"Let me get your feet," he said. He cut through the shoelace holding her ankles together.

Lori sat up and rubbed her ankles while Curt threaded the laces back into her boots. "You're amazing," she said. "I was dropping those papers and making chalk marks, and I kept thinking about Hansel and Gretel. It was like a dumb fairy tale, me leaving little marks for you to follow. But you did it." She grabbed his arm. "Did you see Artie?"

"No problem. He's back down the way, tied up and waiting."

"You really *are* amazing." She gave his arm a squeeze, then let it go. "I thought Artie was dead. Frank had me take his rope and climb this chimney while he went back after Artie. Then when he got up here, he started pulling up the rope. I thought he'd shot Artie. And I figured I was next. So I made my big Wonder Woman move."

"What happened?"

Lori shook her head and smiled. "I blew it. I couldn't keep hold of him. We ended up in a stupid wrestling match, and he was trying to shove me over the edge." Her voice cracked, and she reached out for Curt's arm again. "I jerked loose and pushed him, and he went over. Oh, Curt, I thought I'd killed him."

"I saw the blood on the ledge," Curt said.

"I'm so stupid. He was lying down there, and I started feeling sorry for him. Thought maybe I could save his life or something. So down I went like a moron. And when I got there, he poked the gun in my face. How's that for pure dumb?"

"But how'd you—?"

"I thought he was going to kill me. He was furious. He'd hurt his ankle, and his nose kept bleeding all over the place."

Curt tied her boot and gave her ankle a pat. "You don't have to tell all this—"

"I had to sit down there while he climbed the rope. He had his pistol in his belt. Said he'd stop and shoot me if I moved. Then when he got up here, he made me climb up. I had to untie the rope and get it coiled around him again. He had the pistol in my face every time I came close." Lori took a breath and shook her head. "He wanted to shoot me, but I guess he couldn't get up the nerve. So he tied me up and left me here. And cut the arm off my sweatshirt and stuffed it in my mouth." She shook her head. "I almost choked to death."

Curt patted her ragged sleeve. "Let's get out of here." He swept his light across the floor. "Where's your hat?"

"He threw it back that way." Lori pointed to her left. "But he took the batteries first."

"I have some extras, thanks to Artie." Curt found the hat, put batteries in the pack, and flipped on the light.

"Great," Lori said when he turned the beam of light

toward her. Curt handed her the hat, but she set it aside. "Did I thank you?"

"I don't think so. But you said I was beautiful. I'll settle for that."

"I won't." She reached toward him, pulled him close, and kissed him firmly on the lips. "Thank you."

Curt held her for a long minute, then stepped back. "I'm going to say you're welcome when we have more time."

"Good," Lori said quietly. "What time is it?"

Curt held his watch up to the light. "A little after nine. We can be back in the Cathedral Room by eleven."

"Did you see Pauline?" Lori broke in.

"Yeah. She's fine. Better off than we are. She was wrapped up in her sleeping bag, reading magazines." He looked at his watch again. "We'll get some food there, say hello to Pauline, and go back up the rope. We can still be home a little after midnight."

"It may take longer than that," Lori said. "I'm zonked."

"Me too." He glanced over at her. "You think there's any chance we could find that other way out? Artie said they were supposed to get out by dark, so we must be pretty close."

"It's possible," Lori said. "You saw all those drill marks along the way, didn't you? And the places they cleaned out?"

"All I saw was green chalk and torn-up tickets. But if you know what to look for, let's give it a try."

"It's probably a waste of time," she said. "Frank had a rope with him. He must need it for something."

"Let's risk a half hour," Curt said. "If we don't get anywhere by then, we'll come back here."

Lori shrugged. "I guess there's no danger of catching up with Frank."

"Are you kidding? He's running for his life."

"Not on that ankle. He could barely walk."

Curt waved her away. "He'll manage. He's got two hundred and fifty thousand reasons to keep going."

"I think I know who he is," Lori said. "Before Mom and I moved in, a man with two sons ran the place. I think Frank is one of the sons. Only somebody who lived here could have done all this work."

"Let Quinlan worry about that," Curt said. "I just want to get out of here." He took Lori's hand and helped her up. "The sooner, the better."

Lori led the way with Curt one step behind, marking their path with the green chalk.

After following a meandering passage for several minutes, they reached a dead end. "I know he came this way," Lori said. "I saw a footprint back there."

They retraced their steps, running their lights up the steep walls. Curt spotted a shadow high on the right wall, then noticed a narrow fissure leading down from the shadow. "What do you think?" he asked.

Lori stood back and moved her light slowly up the rock face. "We can make it," she said. "Wait a minute." Her light moved back down a foot. "You see that?"

"What?"

"Right there. I'm circling it. It's a piton."

"A what?"

"A piton. One of those things mountain climbers use. I guess they needed it to get across that space." She turned to Curt. "You ready for this?"

"No, but I'm not ready to go back the way we came either."

"No argument there," she said. "Did you ever hear of the law of three?"

"No."

"It's the climber's law. You've got to keep three things on the rock at all times. Two feet and one hand or two hands and one foot."

"I'll keep that in mind," Curt said.

The law of three was sensible enough, Curt decided after climbing a few feet. But it didn't always work. Sometimes there just weren't places for both feet. And what were you supposed to do when one of your three anchors slipped? He stayed close enough behind Lori so that he could put his hands where her feet had been. Of course, if she fell, she'd take him with her. But he'd bet on her any time.

After he figured that they had already climbed far enough to be at the opening, he began to count movements. He had reached forty-seven when Lori called out, "I'm up." She leaned down and pointed out the last handholds for him. He pulled himself up beside her, then sank down. "It's good to be here," he said.

"Yeah, but where's *here?*"

"We should be almost out."

Lori rubbed her arms. "I hope you're right. I'd hate to have to go back down this thing."

"I was just thinking," Curt said after a minute. "How do you suppose the law of three worked for old Frank if he only had three good ones to start with?"

They made their way through a long, low passage, stooping where they could and crawling where they had to. Lori stopped in front of a small opening and turned back to Curt. "Take a look. Somebody did some blasting in here. You can see by the way the rocks look. So we're still on the right track."

As Curt followed her feet into the tiny opening, he decided that whoever did the blasting stopped much too soon. He had to keep both his arms stretched out in front of him, and his shoulders were still raking both sides.

In the middle of the passage, when the soles of Lori's boots had disappeared from view, Curt thought about her kissing him and broke into a grin. For a minute he forgot how tired and sore he was.

Lori's light flashed in his eyes. "Just a little farther," she called. "It's tight, but you can make it."

Curt's shoulders wouldn't fit through the passage. He shoved one arm ahead and pressed his cheek against his shoulder. He held his other arm flat against his body. Then he pushed forward with his knees.

Lori grabbed his wrist. "Push on three," she said. "One, two, three." His body slid forward. "Again. One, two, three."

He wriggled into a low room. Lori crouched against one wall to give him space. "That's enough of that," he said, rolling onto his side.

"Look what I found." Lori reached behind her and brought out a square of sheet metal.

Curt didn't reach for it. "What is it?"

"A piece of tin. They must have used it to seal off the opening here."

"What for?"

Lori shrugged and set the metal square to one side. "We're getting close," she said. "You ready to go on, or do you want to rest a minute?"

"I want to rest for at least twelve hours, but we might as well go." Curt pushed himself up onto his knees. "You smell something?"

"It's bat guano," Lori whispered.

"What?"

Lori smacked him on the shoulder. "It's okay. The bats are all gone. They go out at night."

"Bats," Curt muttered.

"I'm sure that's why they put the tin over the passage. They didn't want bats getting in there." Lori crawled forward a few feet. "That bat guano isn't exactly perfume, but it's a good sign. We must be almost out."

Curt followed her forward, keeping his light trained on her feet. He was too tired to worry much about bats. He just kept moving ahead, first crawling, then walking with his head ducked low.

The passage led to a small chamber with a ceiling high enough so that he could stand. He kept his head down, not wanting to see what was above him. Three feet in front of him Lori was picking her way through the black muck that covered the floor. Suddenly she spun around and ducked down, throwing her hands above her head. A bat flashed past Curt's ear.

Lori straightened up and grinned. "Scared me."

"I thought you said they were gone at night."

"I guess that one slept late."

The chamber narrowed into a short passage, which turned into another larger chamber. Curt could hear squeaking overhead, but he kept his head down. Lori, he noticed, was doing the same.

The far end of the chamber turned into another passageway. Lori ducked her head and moved her light up and down. Then she reached back for her battery pack. "Turn off your light," she whispered.

Curt rushed up beside her, then flipped off the light. "What did you see?"

"A light." She reached up, took his chin, and turned

it. Far in front of them was a silvery glow. "See it? You know what that is?"

"Frank?"

She squeezed his chin hard. "It's moonlight, Curt. We made it."

Curt reached back and turned on his light. "Let's go."

"Wait a minute," Lori said. "Frank might still be around. Maybe we'd better do this without any lights."

Curt put his hand over his light. He moved his fingers until only a thin beam shone on the ground. "How's that?"

"Lead the way." Lori stepped aside and pushed him forward. She kept her hand on his belt as he headed into the passage.

The passage narrowed as he came closer to the glow. He had to bend over, but at least they didn't have to crawl. His eyes kept moving from the ground at his feet to the glow and then back to the ground. Nothing was moving out there.

When they were almost to the moonlight, Lori gave his belt a yank. She moved close to his ear and whispered, "Let me squeeze past."

"You don't always have to go first," Curt said. He flipped off his light and led the way forward.

He was three steps into the moonlight when the view suddenly opened up into a whole world of stars. "Wow," he said. Warm air struck him in the face.

"Careful," Lori said, no longer whispering. "There may be a dropoff here."

Curt flipped on his light and stepped backward. Two feet in front of him the rock floor ended. Beyond that, everything was dark.

Lori's light flashed on. "I think I see why Frank

brought that rope." She dropped to her hands and knees and crawled across the ledge. "Curt, look! The rope's still here."

He stepped around her and sank to one knee. The rope was looped through a steel link. "Finally something's going right," he said.

The steel link wiggled back and forth.

Curt reached over the side and grabbed the rope. "Lori," he whispered, "he's still on the rope."

12

July 17—10:00 P.M.

"It's perfect," Lori said. "We can haul him in like a big fish." She reached for the rope.

Curt put his hand on her arm. "The fish has a pistol, remember?" He gave her arm a quick squeeze. "Let Quinlan worry about Frank. All we want is the rope." He slid his hand over the side. "There's a big knot here and two ropes. One of them's just hanging loose. You get that one, and I'll get the other. As soon as he lets go, I'll say the word, and we'll yank up both of them."

"Good." Lori settled herself beside him. "We'd better stay back from the edge in case he starts shooting."

Curt wrapped his hand around the quivering rope. "The fish is still on the line," he whispered.

"I still think it would have been fun to—"

"It's gone slack," Curt said. "Get ready."

"Give him a second. Be sure he's clear."

Curt counted to five, then slowly lifted his rope two inches. "Let's go." He yanked the rope upward and sat back on the ledge. He gave the rope another jerk, then began hauling it in a yard at a time.

He and Lori bumped shoulders and elbows while they pulled in rope, which piled up on their laps and around their legs.

"Finally," Lori said when the end of her rope sailed up onto the ledge.

"There's something on the end of mine," Curt said. "I can feel it banging against the rocks."

"Just so it's not Frank." Lori flipped on her light. Near the end of Curt's rope was a metal block. "That's a descender," she said. "It'll make our trip down a lot easier."

Curt shoved the loops of rope off his lap. "He sure had a lot of this stuff."

"He knew what he was doing," Lori said. "You see the way that was tied? You go down one rope, then you pull on the other and haul the whole thing down. Nothing left behind. A few more minutes, and we'd have been sitting up here high and dry."

"I don't want to think about it." Curt leaned back and tried to get comfortable. "We might as well take a rest. We want to give Frank plenty of time to get out of here."

"Maybe we can get him some company," Lori said. "Plug your ears." She cupped her hands around her mouth and screamed, "Help! Help!" She waited a few seconds, then yelled again. She looked over at Curt. "Now it's your turn."

After they had each yelled for help twice, Curt sat back and listened. His throat was dry, and his tongue seemed too big for his mouth. "I've had it," he said. "No more yelling."

"We're somewhere on the back side of the mountain," Lori said. "But you'd think *somebody* could hear us." She yelled once more, then sat back. "It looks like we'll have to rescue ourselves."

"So what's new?" Curt muttered.

While they waited, Lori cut off a piece of rope and

made a harness. When she was finished, she put the harness on Curt and hooked him to the descender. "It's the simplest thing in the world," she said. "You hold it open, and it slides down the rope. You let go, and it stops. And so do you."

"You guarantee that?"

"Move back into the cave and practice with it."

"Things are getting back to normal," Curt said. "You're giving orders again."

"Just try it," she snapped. "I want you to get used to it."

"Yes, boss."

He pulled the rope into the cave and practiced with the descender. The whole process was easier than he had thought.

"Works great," he said when he came back.

"I'm glad you approve," she said sarcastically.

Curt forced himself to laugh out loud. "Hey, don't go getting mad. I'm the guy you thought was beautiful, remember?"

"It was dark in there," Lori said.

Curt crawled past her and peered over the edge. In the moonlight he could make out brush and rocks far below. It was a long way down.

He sat back and looked at his watch. "It's been over half an hour. How long do you want to wait?"

"We could wait till daylight. We'd still have time to get home before anybody there knew anything was wrong. What do you think?"

"You're the boss."

"Knock off that junk," she said.

"Don't be so touchy," Curt said. "I didn't mean it that way."

"I was asking your opinion. Do you want to wait till morning?"

Curt looked up at the stars. "Not really. I've had it with rock mattresses."

"Let's wait another half hour and then go." She turned toward Curt. "Is that all right?"

"Sure."

Lori moved back. "I think I'll go inside where it's cool."

"Go ahead," Curt told her. "I like being where I can see the moon."

When Lori came back, she yelled once more, then started feeding the ropes over the side. Curt stretched out on the ledge and waited. When everything was ready, he grabbed the rope tightly above the descender and rolled off the ledge. The rope slid through his hands until the harness caught him. Lori's light shone down from above his head. "Okay. Now get your hands in place."

Curt moved his left hand onto the handle of the descender, then grabbed the rope with his right. He knew what to do next. He just had to remove the lock with his left hand, then control his speed with his right hand. Any time he let go, he would stop.

But he couldn't make himself remove the lock. He swayed back and forth, bumping against the rock, the ropes cutting into him.

"What's the matter?" Lori asked.

"Nothing."

"It's okay, Curt. Everybody gets scared at first. Just relax and remember how you did it up here."

Curt gritted his teeth. She had used that same sweet, superior tone of voice when he had been stuck in the passage that first time. "Leave me alone," he yelled. "I'm fine." He yanked on the handle.

Twice he stopped to get his balance, but he went on again after a few seconds. He wasn't going to give her time to start yelling advice.

He was surprised when his feet hit the rocks. He was sure that he hadn't come far enough. He held the rope in both hands and tipped his light downward, thinking that he had landed on some kind of outcropping. But he was standing on a pile of rocks, and the scrub oaks began just beyond. He tried to drop to his knees, but the rope held him. He flipped the lock for the last time and plopped onto the ground.

"You looked like a pro," Lori called. "Now take off the harness and tie it to the end of the rope."

Curt waved her away. That was typical of her. He hadn't been on the ground ten seconds, and she was already on his case. He reached down and tugged at the harness. He wouldn't get any peace until she had what she wanted.

Lori took longer to come down the rope than he expected. He was pretty sure he'd done it faster.

"That was kind of fun," she said, slipping out of the harness.

"Beats crawling through caves anyway."

"You know what?" she said. "I'm glad we got out of there before the bats came back. Judging by the floor in there, there must be about a million of them." She wiped her hands on her pants.

"You have any idea where we are?" Curt asked.

"Not exactly. Somewhere on the back side of the ridge."

"So which way do we go?"

"Down," she said. "That's all we can do."

"Let's do it then."

Lori started downhill toward the trees. Curt wondered if there was a stream at the bottom of the hill. If there was, he'd drink out of it. He didn't care what the water looked like. Right then he'd drink out of a mud puddle and be glad for the chance.

"Don't take another step!"

Curt spun around toward the voice. Sitting beside a rock was Frank, framed by their lights. He was holding his pistol in both hands, aiming it at Lori's stomach.

"Put your hands in the air," Frank said. "Now lie down. Flat on your stomachs. Keep your hands over your heads."

Curt did exactly what he was told. A nervous whine in that voice scared him.

"I can't believe you stuck around," Lori said.

"I didn't have much choice. My ankle's as big as a watermelon. You stay right where you are."

Curt raised his head when he heard Frank hopping toward him. "Keep your face in the dirt," Frank shouted. He shoved the cold pistol barrel against Curt's neck. "Where's your gun?"

"I don't have one," Curt said.

The pistol barrel smacked against Curt's skull. "My ankle's killing me," Frank said. "I'm not in the mood for games."

"I don't have a gun," Curt said. "I'm not a sheriff. I just said that."

"No gun? You people are idiots."

"I have a knife in my pants pocket," Curt said.

"Get it with your left hand."

Once Frank had the knife, he hopped backward. "Now roll over. Nice and slow. Keep your hands high."

Curt rolled onto his back. Frank's light shone in his face.

"You're the kid who works at the cave, aren't you?"

"Yeah."

"Followed us all the way. You must be some kind of caver."

Curt snorted.

"Back on your stomach," Frank ordered. "What'd you do with Artie?"

"I tied him up and left him there."

"Poor old Artie. Nothing ever worked out for him." He turned and hopped toward Lori.

"I still don't have anything," Lori said.

While Frank was searching Lori, Curt raised his head just far enough to look around. There was no way to get Frank now. Not while that pistol was pointing at Lori. Curt rested his cheek on the ground. Sooner or later his chance would come.

Frank's light flashed on Curt. "All right, boy. You can turn over now." Curt rolled over, raising his hand to shield his eyes from the light. "What's your name, boy?"

"Curt."

"All right, Curt. I have to get out of here fast, and I can't walk. So you're going to carry me."

Curt let out a moan.

"Before I saw you, I thought we'd have to rig up a stretcher. But you're big enough to carry me piggyback." His light moved from Curt to Lori. "You two are my best chance, but you're not my only chance. If I have to, I'll kill both of you and make myself some crutches. You understand?"

"You'll kill us anyway," Lori said.

"Not unless you make me. Now let's go. Curt, turn your back to me and squat down."

"Let me get rid of my sweatshirt," Curt said. He stripped down to his T-shirt, then turned around and moved into a catcher's crouch.

"Turn your light on," Frank said. "We're going to need all the help we can get." He hopped closer, then shoved the barrel of the pistol into Curt's right ear. "Let's keep everything simple, boy." He wrapped an arm around Curt's neck and sank onto his back. Curt could feel the packets of money pressing against him. "Now get your hands under my legs and stand up. And don't go jerking around. My ankle is killing me."

Curt gritted his teeth as he staggered to his feet. He leaned forward and locked his hands under Frank's legs. It was impossible. He'd be lucky to go a hundred yards with that much weight on his back.

"Lead the way, Lori," Frank said. "Give Curt a break and pick out the easiest path you can."

"I will," Lori said.

"And, Curt, be sensible, all right?"

"Look," Curt said, "you've got to quit choking me. And every once in a while I'm going to have to shift you around."

"Just tell me first," Frank said. "Now let's go."

"Which way?" Lori asked.

"Straight down the hill."

Lori turned and started away.

Frank moved the pistol from Curt's ear to his neck. "Okay, Curt. Hi-yo, Silver."

They spent most of an hour making a wide loop that brought them to the top of the ridge. Lori stayed in front, searching for paths through the brush. Curt stopped to rest every few minutes. He knelt down to let

Frank slide off, then flopped onto the ground. Frank kept whining about his ankle, but Curt was too tired to listen.

From the top of the ridge Curt spotted headlights from a car far off in the distance. Frank didn't mention the lights, but he seemed to know where he was. He had Lori follow the ridgeline for a while, then had her angle off downhill.

Curt couldn't decide whether he hated going downhill or uphill more. Downhill took less energy, but he had to fight for balance. And with Frank's arm wrapped around his neck, he couldn't look down and check his footing.

The only thing that kept him going was the thought of finding a creek at the bottom of the hill. He was going to drink a gallon of water, then soak his head, then drink another gallon. He might even take off his shoes and stick his feet in. Or maybe he'd just slide in, clothes and all.

But the creek was dry. Curt stood on the rocks where the water should have been and looked upstream and down. It wasn't fair. There should have been water in a creek that size. Even in the summer there should have been a little water.

"Let's go," Frank said. He was puffing almost as hard as Curt, and every breath came out as a moan in Curt's ear.

Curt desperately wanted to throw the creep down on the dry creekbed. Soon. Curt's chance would come soon. Frank would make a mistake, and Curt would get that pistol away. Then things would be different. But there still should have been some water in that creek.

They crossed several smaller hills and found dry streambeds at the bottom of each. Then they climbed along an oak-covered sidehill. When Curt saw an open spot, he dropped to his knees. Once Frank slid off his back, Curt pitched forward and lay still.

"We'd better go back and try somewhere else," Lori was saying.

"I'm running out of time," Frank said. "I'm hurting worse than—" Then the voices faded away.

"Curt. Curt." Curt jerked awake, not sure where he was. Lori was kneeling beside him, shaking his shoulder.

"What?"

"We have to go," she said. "You were asleep."

"Let's move," Frank said.

Curt dragged himself to his knees. Frank climbed onto his back, moaning the whole time. Curt sank down again. Frank rammed the pistol barrel into Curt's neck, but Curt was past caring.

"I'll help you," Lori said, wrapping her hands around his upper arm. She pulled him upward, and he staggered to his feet. He took a huge breath, trying to clear his head. It didn't work. His eyes still couldn't focus.

"Let's move," Frank said again.

Lori walked beside Curt, keeping her hands wrapped around his arm. She stopped him at the top of a steep bank. "We can't go straight down," she said. "We'll follow this deer track across to the far side." She ran her light along a narrow trail. Curt saw that the whole bank was crisscrossed with animal trails. "Then we'll cut back again."

"Come on," Frank said. "You can rest at the bottom."

"I'll go right in front of you," Lori told Curt. "Can you get a hand free and hold on to me?"

Curt let go of Frank's right leg and reached for Lori.

"Careful," Frank shouted. His arm dug into Curt's windpipe.

Lori walked too fast, but Curt stayed with her. When they reached the far side, she pointed out the next trail. "You'd better shift hands," she said.

"Just quit running, okay?" Curt leaned forward and used both hands to lift Frank higher. Frank let out a yelp and began to swear. Curt reached for Lori's shoulder with his left hand. She moved ahead slowly, keeping her head bent forward so that she could see her feet.

Halfway across, Curt could feel Frank sliding down his back. He let go of Lori's shoulder and reached back just as Frank yelled, "Wait." Curt tried to step back to get his balance, but his foot slipped, and he went tumbling forward into Lori.

Then he was sliding and rolling. He reached out with his hands, but everything he grabbed was sliding too.

He landed on his back with a thump. Before he could move, the others came crashing down on his stomach. A boot smacked his ribs and something sharp dug into his hip.

"I've got his arm," Lori yelled.

Curt pushed bodies aside and yanked his legs free. His light was out, but Lori's was still on. She was holding Frank's gun arm with both hands while Frank punched her with his free hand. Curt ripped the pistol from Frank's fingers, then shoved him backward.

Still holding the pistol by the middle, Curt stood up and stepped over Lori to get at Frank. When Frank saw him coming, he curled into a ball, wrapping his hands around his head. Curt thought about kicking him once just for the pleasure of it but decided it would take too much effort. He stepped back beside Lori. She was still on the ground, her head bent forward.

Flipping on his light, Curt knelt down beside her. A thin line of blood was running from the corner of her mouth onto her sweatshirt. Her left eye was a deep red, and it was already swelling. He wiped at the blood with his hand and said, "You're amazing."

Lori looked at him and almost smiled. "Yeah. Amazing."

Curt used the tail of his T-shirt to clean her chin. "Remind me never to get in a fight with you."

Lori raised a hand to her eye. "I'll bet this is going to be a beauty."

Curt looked toward Frank, who was now leaning against the bank. "You know what we ought to do to you?"

"Leave him alone, Curt," Lori said.

Curt sighed and sank down onto a rock. "Yes, boss."

"I'm sorry I had to hit you, Lori," Frank said.

Curt snorted. "Terrific. That makes her feel a whole lot better."

"I wasn't going to hurt you," Frank said. "I was going to take you back to the place Artie rented and tie you up. Then when I let people know how to get the cave door open, I was going to tell them where you were. You'd have been big heroes."

Curt reached down and rubbed his sore knees. "Terrific."

"Think about this for a second," Frank said. "New scenario. We go back to the cabin, and I take off in the car. You two wait a few hours, get a little sleep, then come out and say I left you tied and you finally got loose. And for your trouble I leave you fifty thousand dollars. You couldn't spend it for a while, of course, but in a couple of years you could start dipping into it."

"What a cheapskate," Lori said. "He's trying to buy us off with a lousy fifty thousand."

Frank nodded, his light bobbing up and down. "I'm serious. A hundred thousand. Fifty apiece. You can buy a lot of freedom for fifty thousand. You can hide it right around here, and nobody'll ever know."

Curt kept rubbing his knees. It was possible. He wouldn't even have to wait very long to spend it. People would just figure his dad was sending him money from Bolivia. He could get a car, rent an apartment, buy things without counting every quarter.

Nobody would ever know. He'd be crazy not to do it.

Crazy. Just like his crazy father who didn't have a dime, who was working himself to death trying to make life better for other people.

Crazy. But maybe it ran in the family. Because he didn't want it. For years he had complained about being poor, and now that he had a chance for big money, he wasn't interested.

Crazy. And he didn't even care.

"Curt," Lori said, "you're not listening to him, are you?"

"Not me," Curt said. "My boss pays me so well, I wouldn't know what to do with extra money."

"Think about it," Frank said. "Even if I got caught, nobody'd believe you two had anything to do with it."

Lori put her hand on Curt's shoulder. "Let me have the gun."

"What's the matter?"

"Frank has two knives he's going to give us. And if he tries something stupid and has to be shot, I want to be the one to do it."

Curt handed her the pistol. "You earned the pleasure."

"No problem," Frank said. He took the two knives out of his pants pocket and tossed them toward Curt.

Curt stepped forward, scooped up the knives, and stuffed them into his pocket. "Lori," he said, "what do you say we go get an early breakfast?"

"A hundred thousand dollars," Frank said. "Think about it."

"I'd rather think about breakfast," Lori said. Still aiming the pistol at Frank, she lifted her free hand toward Curt. "Help me up." He pulled her to her feet.

"What about me?" Frank asked.

"I'm not carrying you one more foot," Curt said.

"I think I can walk. Give me a chance." Frank crawled over to a rock and pulled himself upright. He stood on one leg for a minute. "I can make it." He bent over his bad ankle, pulling at his pant leg.

"Do you know where we are?" Curt asked Lori.

"More or less. I figure we can get to the road in about fifteen minutes."

"Lori," Frank called out, "shine your light over this way. Be careful. I don't want you to make a mistake."

Lori turned toward him. "What's the matter?"

Frank held out his right hand. "Be real careful," he said. "What I've got here is a hand grenade." He reached up and pulled the pin.

13

July 18—12:30 A.M.

"No!" Lori ran backward several steps and dived to the ground.

Curt dropped onto the rocks and rolled over twice. Banging against a tree trunk, he wrapped his arms around his head and waited for the blast. When it didn't come, he raised his head and looked back toward Frank.

"Take it easy," Frank called out. "Just don't move, and you'll be all right."

"Is that thing a fake?" Lori asked, still edging away.

Frank let out a laugh. "No way. This is U.S. Army issue—made in the U.S.A."

"Then what happened? Why didn't it go off?"

Frank held the grenade in front of his light. "Look at this thing. I want you to understand it. You see the little metal jobs on the sides? They're on a spring. If I let go of them, they'll snap up, and start the fuse. All the pin does is hold them in place. You get it now? As long as I hold this thing tight, everything's cool. If I drop it or throw it, it'll go off in a couple of seconds." He held his hand straight out. "Think about it. I open my fingers, and ka-boom."

"You wouldn't do that," Lori said.

"One more thing. This is an offensive grenade. It

doesn't have that pineapple-looking metal around it. The pineapple ones are defensive grenades. When those things go, they send metal fragments in all directions. So the guy that throws it had better duck behind a wall or something, or he'll get it along with everybody else. But this is different. This just makes a big explosion where it is. So I can toss it in your direction and blow you thirty feet in the air without taking myself out too." He brought his arm back to throwing position. "Do you get the picture?"

"I get it," Lori said.

"Then you'd better bring me the pistol."

Lori took a step back. "No."

"Use your head. That pistol's no help. If you shoot me, I'll drop the grenade, and Curt will be splattered all over the hill."

"I won't shoot you," Lori said. "But I won't let you get any closer either."

Frank swore through closed teeth. When he called to Lori after a minute, his voice was higher. "Look, be sensible. Nobody has to get hurt. We'll go back to my place and get something to eat. You'll be tied up for a little while. Then you'll get rescued, and the whole thing will be over."

"I don't believe you," Lori said.

Frank swore again. "Do something," he said to Curt. "If you don't, I just might kill that idiot for the fun of it."

Curt pulled himself to his knees while he looked around for cover. Couldn't Lori hear the change in Frank's voice? Couldn't she tell he was losing control?

"Use your head," Frank shouted. "All I have to do is throw this, and you're gone."

"If you throw it right."

Frank snorted. "I just have to get it in the neighborhood."

Curt kept his eyes on the grenade as he edged away from the tree.

"Don't you move," Frank screamed. "One more inch, and you're a dead man."

"I won't move," Curt said.

"Careful, Frank," Lori called out. "If you use the grenade on him, what about me?"

"You're an idiot," Frank screamed. "You think you're so smart. You want to spend the rest of your life remembering that this guy got killed because you were stupid?"

"You're not a killer," Lori said quietly. She was still moving away.

"Just watch me," Frank yelled. "Take one more step, and Curt's gone."

"All right," Lori said. "I'll stay right here."

"That's better." Frank reached for the bank with his free hand. "Listen, I can't keep standing here this way. If I sit down, will you sit down too?"

"Do it, Lori," Curt called out.

"Okay." She sat on a rock.

Frank moaned as he slid to the ground. He turned his head toward Curt. "You stay right where you are."

"I'm not going anywhere," Curt said, still on his knees. He had located the best escape route, but the first ten feet were across open ground.

"You wouldn't want to use that on Curt," Lori said. "You'd get yourself too."

"Who cares?" Frank said.

"Come on," Lori called out, "you're not—"

"I don't care anymore." Frank's voice was getting higher. "That's the whole thing. I just don't care—

about anything. For the last three years I've been working at jobs I hate—getting bossed around by idiots,
never making enough money to live on. Who needs it?
I'd rather be dead."

"I see what you're saying," Lori said.

"This was my one chance, see? And you came along
and fouled up everything." Frank's light shifted from
Lori to Curt and back. "Nobody was going to get hurt,
and Ray Thomas wouldn't even miss the money."

"What about Pauline?" Lori said.

Curt bit down hard. Leave it to Lori to say something
like that just when Frank seemed to be calming down a
little.

But Frank laughed. "Her? I can't get too upset about
that poor little rich girl. And her old man—he's got it
coming. Let that slimeball squirm a little for a change."

"What did he ever do to you?" Lori asked.

Frank laughed again. "Oh, nothing. Nothing at all."
He turned his light on Lori and shouted. "All he did was
kick me out of my home and wreck my family." He
cocked the arm holding the grenade. "Listen, I could
have killed his daughter, and we still wouldn't be
even."

"I'm sorry," Lori shouted. "I didn't know."

"There's a lot you don't know," Frank said, no longer
yelling. "I used to live in your house—did you know
that?"

"Really?"

Frank lowered his arm. "That's right. Me and my
brother Don and my father. We were the ones who got
that cave ready to open—blasted out the paths, put in
the lights, did all the paving. And Don and I found that
hole in the Pink Room. We spent all our time off—
months and months—exploring in there. We were hop-

ing to find a really great room—like the Cathedral Room, only better. Something to make us famous. But we never got lucky." He jerked his light over to Curt, then turned back to Lori. "You saw what it's like in there. It's okay, but it's not going to make anybody famous."

"Yeah," Curt said. He now had his feet underneath him, and he was moving into a sprinter's crouch.

"And then we found that way out. We did a lot of clearing, and we had to blast some, but we ended up with a new way out that nobody knew about—not even my dad."

"What does Thomas have to do with this?" Lori asked.

"That fat toad came along and bought the whole thing. He didn't care about the cave. He was just buying land, figuring on developing it someday. Then one day he came through on a cave tour without even saying who he was. The next day he sent some flunky out to fire my dad. Didn't like the way things were being run, so he canned us. Didn't give us a chance to explain or anything."

"I see why you hate him," Lori said.

"Do you?" Frank yelled. "Do you really? Then you don't need to hear about my father turning into a bum and my brother killing himself on a stolen motorcycle." He raised the grenade again.

"I'm sorry," Lori called out.

"They just quit caring—both of them. Nothing mattered." His hand dropped into his lap. "I didn't understand it then, but I do now." He shook his head. "My brother's dead, and I don't even know where my father is. So don't expect me to start feeling sorry for Ray

Thomas because his little girl spent a couple of nights in a cave."

"I'm sorry," Lori said again.

"Lousy luck," Frank said quietly. "That's the whole story. Last summer I read an article in the newspaper about Thomas—a bunch of garbage about what a great guy he was—how he didn't want his kids to have it too easy, how he had his daughter working for wages as a tour guide. That gave me the idea. And it should have worked. I was the only person alive who knew about that opening. Don and I had plugged it up with rocks so nobody would find it by accident. It was perfect. Can't you see that?"

"Sure," Curt said, keeping his eyes on the hand grenade. Frank was twisting it around like a baseball. He seemed to have forgotten he was holding it.

"Lousy luck. I did everything right. You never saw me, but I knew your whole schedule. And it would have worked. If you hadn't been such idiots, we would have been gone with the money, and it might have been years before anybody figured out how we did it." He reached up and scratched his ear with the hand that was holding the grenade.

"Be careful with that thing," Curt said.

Frank looked at Curt, then at the grenade. "Right. The way my luck's been going, I might drop it by accident." He shook his head. "Think about it. Perfect plan, but I just didn't have any luck."

"Yeah," Curt said. "How could you know I was following you? And I happened to catch Artie with his feet sticking out of a hole."

"You can't fight luck," Frank said. "Not with all the planning in the world."

"It should have worked," Curt said.

Frank sneered in Curt's direction. "Don't start feeling sorry for me. I'm not finished." He turned his head toward Lori. "All right, use your head. Why should anybody get hurt here? If I get away, so what? What difference does it make to you whether I'm in Mexico or in jail?"

Lori stood up. "None."

"So bring me that pistol, and let's get going."

Lori took several quick steps backward. "I can't do that," she called out.

"Bring it here right now," Frank shouted.

Lori kept backing away. "I can't."

"You want me to kill Curt?"

Curt had his weight on the balls of his feet, ready to move the second he saw a chance.

"You won't do that," Lori said.

"Not unless you make me," Frank yelled. "It'll be your fault."

"You're not a killer," Lori called. Her light was growing fainter.

"Bring me that gun."

"It's too late," Lori said. "Put the pin back in the grenade, so we can get you some help for your leg." Her light disappeared. Curt couldn't tell whether she had turned it off or had stepped behind something. Frank's light swung in his direction.

"She ruined it all," Frank said quietly. "The whole perfect plan—blown to pieces by one stupid girl."

"Rotten luck," Curt said, keeping his eye on the grenade.

"She's too dumb to think things through. She should never have come into the cave in the first place. And look at things now. If she gets you killed, it'll wreck her whole life. But she can't think that far ahead." He took a noisy breath. "So I end up ruined because she's too stupid to do what makes sense."

"You can still make it," Curt said.

"You can't fight luck. Some people are born lucky, and some aren't. And a lot of people never have the guts to find out which they are." His head sagged forward, and his light shone on the ground in front of him. "At least I gave it a try."

Curt planted his rear foot, like a sprinter at the starting blocks. "Things can work out. You've still got the money, and I can carry you just like before."

Frank kept staring at the ground. "It's too late now. She'd have the police after me, and I can hardly— It's too much. You know what I mean? My foot aches so bad, and I'm exhausted. And I just don't care." He looked at Curt. "That's the real bottom line. I just don't care anymore."

Curt saw Frank's hand drop, and he knew what was going to happen next. The grenade slid from Frank's fingers, and Frank dropped on top of it.

Curt was already moving forward. He caught Frank's shoulder and threw him back. Planting his left foot, Curt scooped up the grenade and gave it the quick flip he used for a downcourt pass.

Then the world exploded.

14

July 18—12:45 A.M.

His ears hurt. That was the first thing Curt realized. His ears ached, and the pain was seeping into his forehead. He was lying on his back, but he didn't know how he had gotten there. He was afraid to move. If part of him was blown away, he didn't want to know it.

"Curt! Curt!" Lori was holding him, shining her light in his face. "I'm so sorry."

He tried to say, "Come back later," but the words got jumbled in his mouth.

"Can you move your legs?" she asked.

He wasn't even sure that he still had legs, but he wiggled enough to satisfy her.

Next came his hands. And then she was pulling open his eyelids and trying to blind him with her light.

"I'm all right," he said, trying to push her aside. "Just let me rest a second."

"Okay." She turned her light on his face again and stroked his cheek. "I still think you're beautiful."

By the time Curt was ready to try standing up, Lori had Frank tied to the trunk of a tree. "I can go get help for you," she told Curt.

"I'll make it," he said. "I'm just a little shaky."

"You'll have to wear Frank's hat," she told him. "Your light got smashed."

When the hat was in place and the light was turned on, Curt walked over to where Frank was lying.

Frank looked up at him. "See?" he said. "No luck at all."

It took Curt and Lori most of an hour to reach the highway. They had to cross two ravines and weave their way across brushy hillsides. Curt plodded along behind Lori, paying no attention to where he was going. With his aching head and ringing ears, he just wanted to lie down and close his eyes.

When they finally stumbled out onto the highway, they sat down on the smooth pavement. After a few minutes, Lori looked at Curt. "You wait here. I'll go get the car."

"You're giving orders again," Curt said.

Lori smiled and shook her head. "I'm sorry. It's a habit."

"A dumb habit."

"I can't help it. I get bossy when I'm nervous and scared."

"So quit being nervous and scared."

"Yes, boss," she said.

Curt glanced around. "You know where we are?"

"Yeah. For the first time in a long time. We're about half a mile from the cave turnoff."

"Then let's go," Curt said.

Lori swept her light across his face. "You don't have to."

"I came this far with you. I'm not about to quit now."

They turned off their lights and walked down the road in the moonlight. Curt tried to stay on the white centerline, but he kept drifting to one side or the other.

"It's silly," Lori said, "but I feel kind of sorry for Frank."

"Wait till you get a look in the mirror," Curt said. "When you see your eye, you may change your mind."

"You know what I mean, don't you? Even with all he did, don't you feel a little sorry for him?"

"I guess so." He took a deep breath. "But he's not on the top of my list. I feel sorrier for Pauline. And Artie. And I feel sorry for me. I don't feel so good right now."

"Sit down and rest. I can be back here with the car in a few minutes."

"I'll make it. Just don't start—"

"You don't have to say it," Lori told him. "I'll shut up."

When they reached the spot where they had left the Chevrolet, Lori flipped on her light and shone it into the trees. The car was still sitting where they had left it. "You want a ride?" she asked.

"I'd rather walk," Curt said. "I want to walk right up to the cabin and see what those morons are doing. We scream for help, and Frank sets off a bomb, and nobody pays any attention."

"I'm with you," Lori said, turning off her light. "It's hard to believe we were here last night."

Curt sighed. "Seems like last year."

A white car was parked across the entrance to the cave turnoff. Curt wondered if the same bored-looking deputy was sitting behind the wheel.

Lori moved close to Curt. "What do you think?"

"About what?"

"Do we talk to the guy in the car?"

"Let's go around," Curt said. Right then he didn't want to talk to anybody. All he could think about was the water fountain outside the store. The other things could wait. Somebody would have to go into the cave and get Pauline. And the door was still booby-trapped. And who would go after Artie? And they'd probably need a stretcher for Frank. But first came the water fountain.

They moved into the trees and made a wide circle that brought them to the cave road thirty yards past the car. "We'd better stay in the shadows," Lori whispered.

"Too much trouble." Curt headed down the middle of the road. The water fountain was getting close now.

When they were almost to the parking lot, Lori pulled on Curt's arm. "How do you want to handle this?"

"Water first," Curt said.

"Good idea."

They walked straight through the lighted parking lot, past vans from the television stations and white cars from the sheriff's office. The only sound they could hear was from the air conditioner in the store.

Curt bent over the drinking fountain, braced himself against the wall of the store, and lowered his mouth to the water. He drank and drank and still couldn't get enough. He pushed himself back to give Lori a chance, but the minute she moved, he was over the fountain again. When he couldn't drink any more, he slid down to the ground.

"They're all asleep," Lori whispered. "Under the stupid air conditioner. No wonder they didn't hear us." She put a hand in the fountain, then rubbed the water on her face and neck. "I think we ought to talk to Sheriff Quinlan first. Anybody else, and we'll just have to tell it over again."

Curt looked up at her. "I think you're going to have to tell it," he said, but the words didn't come out right.

A frightened look crossed Lori's face. "I'm just tired," he tried to say, but "tired" stuck to his tongue. It didn't matter. Lori would know what he meant.

His head was too heavy to hold up any longer. He let it slide sideways, and the ground came up to meet it. Somewhere, far away, Lori was yelling, "Get a doctor," and he wondered if she had hurt herself. His ears were still ringing.

15

Curt walked out of the storeroom with the basketball in his left hand. He was exhausted. That morning they had reopened the cave, and tourists had flocked in. Curt had started the day behind the counter, Wanda figuring that he should still take it easy. But after a morning of answering questions, posing for pictures, and signing autographs, he had insisted on leading tours to get a little rest.

The doctors had kept him in the hospital for two days, mostly for exhaustion. By the time he was alert enough to ask what was going on, everything was finished. Sheriff Quinlan had immediately sent a party after Frank, figuring that Frank could tell them how to open the cave door. But Ray Thomas didn't trust those instructions, and Quinlan ended up sending in a demolition team through Lori's opening. The team had found Pauline eating peaches and reading *Cosmopolitan.* She said her only problem was eyestrain from reading in bad light.

A group of cavers from another county had gone in after Artie and brought him out just in time to make a full confession, live, on the six o'clock news. Compared with that confession, the televised shots of Curt lying in a hospital bed were pretty dull. So much for show business.

The story had even reached Bolivia. Curt's father had telephoned, asking if he should come. Once Curt had reassured him and promised a letter with all the details, they had both gone silent. "Well, I'd better let you go," Curt had said. "This call's probably costing you ten dollars a minute."

"Yeah," his father had said. Then, "I'm proud of you, son."

He had hung up before Curt could figure out how to tell him the same thing. Now Curt would have to try to put it in the letter.

Since coming home from the hospital, Curt had done nothing but lie around and eat Wanda's cooking. He had probably gained ten pounds.

He dribbled lazily to the left and flipped a hook shot toward the basket. It bounced off the front rim.

"Lousy form," Lori called from behind him.

"Give me a break, Coach. I just got out of the hospital." Curt jogged after the rebound and tossed her the ball.

"Always some excuse." Lori stood in the same spot, dribbling slowly. "Pauline called. She wants to work tomorrow."

"Good. We can use her."

"She's been talking to a psychiatrist, and even he thinks she ought to come back if she wants to."

"I hope you told her to expect a madhouse."

"I told her. She doesn't care. She's bored sitting around home." Lori stopped dribbling and threw him the ball. "You know what else she said? She said some group from New York called her father today. They want to buy the cave or set up a partnership or something. They want to change the name—call it Kidnap Cave or some garbage like that—and make a big deal out of it. Pauline said they want to make a movie and use it as part of the tour."

Curt tossed the ball back to her. "Kidnap Cave. You think it'll happen?"

"It might. It's crazy enough to work." She dribbled slowly to her right, then stopped and held the ball. "They'll probably get some little Hollywood starlet to play me in the movie."

"What's the matter? Don't you want to be a movie star?"

"That's not the point. I just don't look like a girl who needs rescuing. I don't think the world's ready for a six-foot-two princess."

"It's their loss," Curt said, holding out his hands for the ball.

Lori threw it to him. "I'll tell you one thing. You and I are going to be seeing a few recruiters this fall. Every time they turned the TV camera on me, I told them that you and I were basketball players looking for the right college. That kind of publicity never hurts."

"I'm glad they're not here now," Curt said. "I'm a little rusty."

"You big faker. Listen to you preparing your alibi. I can hear it all now." She coughed twice and said in a whine, "I woulda won, but I've been sick."

Curt laughed and bounced the ball in front of him. "Are you going back to that stuff? What happened to the girl in the cave who was kissing me and saying I was beautiful?"

"You're really playing dirty now."

"Am I supposed to forget all that? Pretend it didn't happen?"

Lori shrugged. "I don't know. It might be smarter that way."

"Then I must be dumb. I can't see us going back to being two guys playing roundball. Can you?"

Lori looked him in the eye. "Not necessarily. What do you have in mind?"

Still holding the ball in his hand, Curt took a step toward her. "A few minutes ago I was thinking about kissing you. Now I'm not so sure I want to."

Lori reached out and squeezed his shoulder. "You'll probably get in the mood again."

Curt put his hand over hers. "It's possible."

"I'll tell you what," she said. "If you want to kiss me, you'll have to beat me first." She knocked the ball out of his hand and dribbled to her left.

He moved back toward the basket. "What if you win?"

"Then *I* kiss *you*." She faked with her head, dribbled around him, and made an easy lay-up. "Two–zip. Let's go."

About the Author

P. J. Petersen was born in Santa Rosa, California, and grew up on a farm in Sonoma County. He attended Stanford University, San Francisco State University, and the University of New Mexico, from which he holds the doctorate in English.

He is the author of many books for young readers, including *Would You Settle for Improbable?* and *Nobody Else Can Walk It for You,* both American Library Association Best Books for Young Adults.

P. J. Petersen lives with his wife and two daughters in Redding, California, where he teaches English at Shasta College.